Silent Night

A Christmas Story Collection

WENDY CLARKE

For permission requests, email:
editor@cobblestonewalkpublishing.co.uk

Published by Cobblestone Walk Publishing

First published 2017

.

Author: Wendy Clarke

http://wendyswritingnow.blogspot.co.uk

ISBN: 9781549770043

'Silent Night' is a collection of thirteen stories of family and friendship by Wendy Clarke, a regular writer of fiction for national magazines.

All of these stories have previously been published in either 'The People's Friend' or 'Take a Break Fiction Feast'. If you like stories with emotional depth and a satisfying ending, then this collection is for you.

'Wendy Clarke has become one of The People's Friend's most valued writers, offering our readers a range of themes and a level of emotional satisfaction that is rare in the short story format.'

Shirley Blair

Commissioning Fiction Editor for 'The People's Friend'

CONTENTS

Project Christmas   1

On My Own   13

Silent Night   27

A Christmas Present Called Abbie   35

Do You Believe in Angels   49

A Song for Christmas   57

The Memory Purse   71

All I Want for Christmas   85

Cancelling Christmas   95

The Greatest Gift   107

Christmas Strike   115

Finding Santa   129

Together for Christmas   141

PROJECT CHRISTMAS

This Christmas everything must be the same as it's always been.

That was the thought which filled Andrew's head as he sat on the edge of his son's bed and watched his eyes flicker in sleep. Pulling the duvet a little higher over the child's thin shoulders, he smoothed Nicholas' fringe from his forehead, leant over and kissed his brow. It was something he found difficult to do when Nick was awake.

The boy turned over and murmured something in his sleep and Andrew stood up, afraid that he might wake. It had been a while now, thankfully, since Nick had had one of his nightmares. He found it hard to admit but in the early months after his wife, Paula, had died, he hadn't known what to do for the best when his son had cried out in the night. The boy missed his mum. They all did.

'Dad!' Now Mattie was awake.

Leaving Nick, Andrew crossed the landing to his daughter's room. The night-light, with its Disney Princesses dancing across the shade, cast a soft glow over the room.

'What is it, Mattie?'

'I can't sleep. I can't find Pink Rabbit.'

Fishing down the side of his daughter's bed, he found the worn toy, its stuffing working its way out of the faded pink fabric. He handed it to her. This was something he could do. Something practical. He wasn't very good at the rest of the parenting bit. It was hard to cope with the children's grief as well as his – trying to find answers to their questions when he had so many unanswered of his own.

He and Paula had met in their second year at university. He had been a member of the rugby club while she was president of the debating society, but despite their different interests, they had hit it off straight away. He had asked her on a date and soon they were seeing each other regularly.

Paula had made it clear, right from the start, that having children would be part of her future, with or without him. Three years later, as he asked her to marry him, Andrew was equally clear that if she wanted children he was all for it – but he would leave all the nurturing stuff to her.

'How many more days till Christmas comes, Daddy?'

It was a question Mattie had asked every night since the first advert, involving a can of fizzy drink and a walking Christmas tree, had graced their television screen.

'Not for another month or so, Mattie.'

The little girl frowned. 'Is that a big amount?'

Just as Andrew was struggling to think how Paula would have explained it, Mattie took his hand and touched his fingers. It was as if she had read his thoughts. 'How many sleeps?'

'Oh, I see. Thirty sleeps, Mattie. That's how long.' Although she could not count that far, Mattie seemed happy with the answer. 'Will we have decorations and that rolly log thing?'

A picture came into Andrew's mind of Mattie sitting up on the work top next to Paula, her hands clasped around the wooden spoon with which she was stirring some chocolaty mixture.

'Of course.'

Putting her thumb in her mouth, and clutching Pink Rabbit to her chest, Mattie closed her eyes and it wasn't long before she was asleep.

Their first Christmas without Paula. The thought made his heart ache. He didn't know how he was going to do it, but he had made up his mind that, whatever happened, he would try and make it the same as it had always been. For the children's sake... for all their sakes.

The only problem was that Christmas had always been his wife's domain – just as the children had been. Apart from stringing the lights up under the eaves of the house and carving the Christmas turkey, Paula had been happy for him to leave the bulk of it to her. Now it was down to him alone.

What I need is a list, he thought. It was a practical start. If he worked through it, methodically, and tried not to be sidetracked by thoughts of Paula singing to the radio as she stirred the pudding, or tickling him as he stretched up to put the star on top of the tree, he would be able to do it. He was a project manager, after all. Well, he used to be – now his days were spent taking the children to school and doing all the jobs Paula had once done to keep the family going. Yes, that's what he'd do. He'd made up his mind – this would be his project.

Going downstairs to the room he used as an office, he took a piece of paper from the printer and in bold pen wrote PROJECT CHRISTMAS at the top. Underneath, he added some numbers then began to write.

1. Buy presents
2. Decorate house
3. Buy tree
4. Make rolly log thing Paula used to make

It didn't seem very much – there must be more to it. Maybe he'd ask his sister, Beth. She was good at this sort of thing – better than he was anyway. Putting down the pen, he looked around him. The house was quiet; he still couldn't get used to not hearing Paula's voice talking about her day or telling him off for leaving his shoes in the hall. He would leave all his shoes in the hall just to hear her voice again.

Picking up his list, he went into the living room and switched on the television. An old 1950s film had just started – a family sitting around a huge Christmas tree, opening their presents while the snow fell softly outside the window. A perfect Christmas Day, like the ones Paula used to organise. As he watched, the family gathered round the piano and, as the wife played, they all began to sing Christmas carols. No, he wouldn't ask Beth for help; it was down to him to make this Christmas just as perfect in his wife's memory.

Andrew switched the television off again, then sat in the silent living room, his head in his hands.

'I don't think you should interfere, Beth.' Keith looked up from his paper. 'He might not thank you for it.'

'It's not interfering. He's my brother and I just want to make sure everything's all right.'

Beth walked over to the Christmas tree in the corner of the living room and replaced a bauble that had dropped onto the floor. The tree hosted a gaudy mix of home-made decorations that the children had made when they were younger, and an assortment of end of season baubles bought in the New Year sale. What a contrast to her sister in law's house where the decorations were all colour co-ordinated. Paula had always been artistic and the decorations she made each year could have graced any high-end craft shop. She sighed. Things would be very different this year. Picking up her car keys and bag, she walked to the door.

'I won't be long. It's not right that Andrew is doing all this on his own. I'll just check there isn't anything I can do – or better still, persuade him to come over to ours Christmas day.'

'Well, don't blame me if he gives you short shrift. He seemed pretty adamant that he wanted to go it alone when we last spoke to him.'

Beth frowned. 'I know he did… but still.'

Although not yet four o'clock, it was getting dark as Beth started the car and drove across town to her brother's house. Most of the houses had trees in their windows and a few had chasing lights strung along the edges of their roofs.

It had always been a tradition in Andrew and Paula's household that they wouldn't decorate the house until the weekend before Christmas and then Paula would go into overdrive, cutting and sticking and baking until the house was transformed into a tasteful wonderland. Anyone lucky enough to come to the door that weekend would probably be greeted by the delicious chocolatey aroma from her speciality yule log.

How would Andrew be coping? Her numerous offers of help, over the last few weeks, had been rejected. *I have it under control*, he had said. She wanted to believe him – for all their sakes.

Beth stared at the scene before her. The room looked like a bomb had hit it. The floor was littered with scraps of gold and silver paper and there was the unmistakeable smell of burning chocolate cake coming from the oven. Stooping down, she picked up a tube of glue. The lid was nowhere to be seen but its contents were a snail-trail across the stripped-pine floor. Her brother sat at the kitchen table a glass of beer in his hands – the children were nowhere to be seen.

'Is everything okay, Andrew? Where are the children?'

Andrew stared dejectedly into his beer. 'I sent them upstairs. They kept trying to help but you can see what happened.' He swept an arm around the room in explanation.

'I thought I could do it, Beth.' Picking up a glitter-covered paper snowflake which had got stuck to another, he crushed it in his fist. 'But I can't.'

Beth stood beside her brother and put an arm around his shoulder. 'Don't be so hard on yourself, Andy. You're doing great.'

Andrew shook his head. 'Call this great? If Paula could see this…'

She looked at him and saw the lines between his brows. He would be beating himself up about this just like he had as a child when, despite following the instructions on the box, he couldn't get the last Lego pieces to fit, or as a teenager when he couldn't reach the next level on his game of Dungeons and Dragons.

'If Paula could see this, she would think what a marvellous job her husband is doing. It's been less than a year, Andrew. You can't expect it to be easy.'

'I made a list,' he said, and the hopelessness in his voice made her want to weep.

'Show me.'

Andrew picked up a page of printer paper and handed it to her. She looked at it then raised her eyebrows. 'Project Christmas?'

'I thought it would help.'

Beth ran her finger down the list. 'Buy presents. Well… did you?'

Andrew shook his head. 'I hadn't a clue what anyone would want. Paula did all that.'

'What everyone would want would be to see you happy again.' She screwed the lid on the tube of glue. 'I see you made a start with number two. What about the tree? Did you buy it?'

'Nothing left worth getting,' Andrew shrugged. 'I remembered too late that Paula used to order one from the garden centre. The only ones they had when we got there were either seven foot tall or hardly big enough to hang anything on – though looking at my decoration failure, that wouldn't be such a bad thing.'

'I'd better rescue this.' Beth got the oven gloves and bent to take out the cake of the oven. It was dark brown around the edges but the centre seemed to be all right. 'What were you going to do with this?'

'Make the chocolate rolly log thing, Paula used to do.'

'I see. Well, I don't think that's going to work now but we can salvage a lot of it and make it into something else.'

'But it's what Paula always makes.' He stared down at his hands. 'Made.'

Beth turned away so that her brother couldn't see the tears in her eyes. She turned the cake out onto a cooling rack and when she turned back she had a determined look on her face.

'Right, that's enough.' She walked purposefully to the door.

Andrew looked up. 'What are you doing?'

'I'm getting the kids.' Standing at the bottom of the stairs, Beth called out. 'Nick... Mattie. Can you come downstairs a minute, darlings.'

Mattie was first into the room, clutching Pink Rabbit firmly under her arm, followed soon by Nick. The little girl climbed onto her father's lap and Beth smiled as she watched Andrew drop a kiss onto her fair head.

'It's all right to ask for help, sometimes, bro, and who better to ask than us? Come on – we'll do to together.'

8

'Budge up.' Andrew waited for Nicholas to move across, then sat on the bed next to him. 'I want to talk to you.'

'And me.' Mattie stood at the door, Pink Rabbit in her hand.

'I thought you were asleep.'

'I couldn't sleep, I was too excited.'

Andrew smiled and patted the bed next to him. 'There's still three sleeps to go, Mattie. Come on then. There's room enough for us all.' He lifted Mattie up and she snuggled up to him. Smiling, he put an arm around both his children. 'You know we've done all right, haven't we?'

Nick nodded. 'I like the tree. We've never had a silver one before.'

After his sister had given him his talking to, they had got their coats and driven to the nearest garden centre. Despite there being many realistic green trees, the children had fallen in love with this one straight away.

'I liked making the chocolate cake stars with the cutty things.'

'Yes, it was kind of Aunty Beth to go home and get them for us, wasn't it?'

Beth had put on some Christmas music and they had spent what was left of the day making paper chains and an assortment of mismatched tree decorations, dripping with glitter and glue. They had worked together and, as Andrew and Nick had watched Mattie trying to lick the icing sugar off her nose with the tip of her tongue, he'd realised it was the first time they had laughed properly since Paula had died.

'I have an idea,' Andrew said. 'It's a bit short notice but shall we ask Auntie Beth and Uncle Brian to have Christmas with us?'

'Yes please… and Pink Rabbit.' Mattie snuggled into him and Andrew laughed. Christmas wouldn't be easy for any of them without Paula but they would do the best they could to fill it with love and hope – together as a family. It would be a different sort of Christmas but, it would be their own… and one he knew Paula would have been proud of.

ON MY OWN

'I'm not going through another Christmas like last year's.' I try not to raise my voice but I can feel a hysterical note creeping in.

'Look Bella, it's just one day out of three hundred and sixty-five.'

I know Ryan is making a super human effort to keep his temper as well but just this once I want to try doing things my way.

'It's not any old day, Ryan. It's Christmas day and we're not talking about just one day either, are we. Keeping everyone happy is going to take at least three days.'

Ryan comes over to me and strokes my hair in that annoying way he has when he's trying to persuade me to do something. I bat his hand away and continue wrapping the presents: a garden token for Dad and Peggy, a theatre voucher for Mum and Morris, a day's golfing for Ryan's dad and…I realise that I haven't got anything for his mum yet.

'I remember when we bought proper presents for people – you know, photo frames and picnic hampers and ornaments and stuff.'

'You mean you want me to buy you an ornament for Christmas?'

'You know I don't mean that. It's just that it's all so impersonal now.' I wave a hand at the collection of envelopes that I've wrapped in shiny red paper. 'When I was a child, Christmas was so simple and magical. All it is now is three days playing piggy in the middle, trying to please everyone.'

'It'll be fine, Bella. We managed to see everyone last year; we can do it again. It just needs a little planning, that's all. I could do a spread sheet.'

At first I think Ryan is joking but when he gets up and crosses to the computer, I realise he is deadly serious. This Christmas, like the others, will be planned like a military operation. A shiver of irritation runs down my spine.

For the last three years, since we moved in together, we have been juggling our families at Christmas. How I wish we could be one of those modern families you read about, who all gather together amicably over the festive period, forgetting their differences. I chuckle to myself as I try to imagine Mum and Peggy sipping a sherry together or Dad and Morris exchanging views on current affairs. That's without adding Ryan's family into the equation.

It's not that I don't get on with his parents: his dad's okay, if you share his interest in golf and his mum – well – it's just that I would rather not have to sit through her asking Ryan once again when he's going to make an honest woman of me.

Ryan is at the computer. He looks over his shoulder at me to make sure that he has my full attention.

'I think if we invite your dad and Peggy over for supper on Christmas Eve, say around six, we can then have my mum over too and she can stay the night and have lunch with us on Christmas day.' He is looking particularly pleased with himself and I suppress an urge to throw something at him.

'What about my mum and Morris? You know they were hinting that they wanted to have Christmas lunch with us this year. Your mum was with us last year after all.' I'm suddenly feeling very tired. Only a month to go and I'm already wishing the whole thing was over. 'And your dad – we can't expect him to settle for Boxing Day again – that will be three years in a row.'

Ryan looks smug. 'I have put Dad in at nineteen hundred hours for cheese and biscuits on Christmas day – Mum will have left by then. Now where can we fit in your mum and Morris?' I watch him consulting his spread sheet; never has the ten-year age gap seemed so vast. 'Maybe for pre-lunch drinks or how about boxing day lunch?'

'But when are we going to have time for ourselves, Ryan?' I know I'm sounding whiney – Ryan hates that. I see his brow furrow. 'We haven't spent time alone together at Christmas since…I don't know when. Let's just go away somewhere. A little cottage on Dartmoor or, even better, by the sea. Just image Christmas Eve, snuggling up by a log fire, the snow falling. We could take a Christmas tree and that CD of carols. '

'Don't you think you're getting just a little carried away?'

Ryan comes back over to me, shaking his head as if at a wayward child. He raises his hand to stroke my hair again and I vow that if he does, I will go away on my own. I will stay in that cottage.

'So, what are you going to get my mum?' he asks as I feel his hand on the top of my head.

I almost miss the turning to the hamlet of Trethey as the wipers are fighting a losing battle against the rain and the windscreen has misted up. I wipe an arc across the screen with my sleeve and peer at the weathered sign. The lane is small and the bare branches of the hedges close in on either side of the car.

The sat nav tells me to do a u-turn. Stopping again, I struggle to read the instructions I have been sent by the owner Patricia Turner. *Turn right at the sign to Trethey. Drive through the village and turn left at the bakery. Sea Crest Cottage will be up a short unmade lane on the right.* Yes, this is definitely the right way.

I'm pretty sure that the term *village* flouts the trade descriptions act as it consists only of a huddle of grey houses straggling out along the narrow road. The bakery on the corner appears to be closed and 'The Green Man' public house hunkers down – doors firmly closed against the unwelcome weather. After a four hour drive, I am not amused.

The unmade lane turns out to be barely more than a track with rivers of water flowing down either side of a series of potholes. I am so busy trying to avoid a puncture that the cottage appears suddenly.

The picture on the internet site had shown a stone cottage with a small garden. Of course, the photo had been taken in the summer when the sky was blue and the garden ablaze with flowers but it is still hard to imagine that this is the same place. With the paint peeling on its door and window frames, it looks sad and neglected in the December rain. It's two days before Christmas and already I am beginning to feel I may have made a terrible mistake.

Grabbing my holdall from the passenger seat, I cover my head with my raincoat and make a dash for the front door. The key is where I have been told it will be – under the doormat. As I let myself in, the first thing I notice is the smell of damp. Dropping my bag on the scuffed linoleum, I run back for the rest of my things: a box of food, a carrier stuffed with tinsel, paper chains and fairy lights and the old Christmas tree I had at university. Ryan would be horrified. Every year we buy our non-drop blue spruce from Simmon's Garden Centre. I'm pretty sure Ryan thinks the sky will cave in if we buy it from anywhere else.

I notice, as I stand dripping in the dark hallway, that the walls are covered in a series of small water colours. In one, a fishing boat is leaning drunkenly on the pebbles of a beach; in another, great waves are breaking against black rocks. There are others too, simply framed, the theme always the same: great expanses of sea and sky, rocks and beaches. I am no connoisseur but whoever painted these pictures has talent.

I think of the garden room at the back of my mother's house where, as a teenager, I had loved to experiment with watercolours – unsure of who I was and what I was trying to create. Years later, Ryan had smiled indulgently when I told him of my hobby and said that once we moved in together we would be able to buy our own artwork. I realised, soon enough, that a messy art studio would not be part of the deal.

Remembering that the advert had boasted breathtaking views from the upstairs windows, I run up the narrow staircase and into the larger of the two rooms but the rain is battering against the window making it impossible to see anything.

The springs squeak as I sit heavily on one of the twin beds. What to do now? The advert said the cottage was an ideal base for exploring spectacular cliff top walks and picturesque harbours but in this rain the idea isn't so appealing. The pink candlewick bedspread beneath my legs, reminds me of the bedroom of my childhood and I feel an unsettling pang of homesickness, although it is five years since I lived in my parents' house. I look at my mobile – no signal – now there's a surprise.

Deciding that a cup of tea might help cheer my spirits, or maybe even a glass or two of the Chablis I've brought with me in the cool bag, I make my way back to the kitchen and start to empty the food bag. It's then that I notice the note propped up against the tea caddy.

Dear Bella

Sorry I wasn't here to greet you when you arrived but I'm at a show. I've turned the heating on for you, so it should be warm.

Please make yourself at home. I have left information sheets on the dresser in the kitchen and you'll find plenty of things to do in the cupboards under the bookshelves in the sitting room — If you're feeling creative.

I will pop in to make sure all is well when I get back.

Pat

I wonder if the show is a local pantomime and if there is a brochure for it amongst the information sheets but these are nowhere to be seen. I shiver and feel the radiator. It is stone cold. Pat has obviously not turned on the heating, as she said she had. This is disconcerting. With Ryan as its foreman, I am used to a house that runs like a well-oiled machine.

After making a mental note to write a bad review on the cottage web site, I pull my jumper around me and take my tea into the living room.

Propping the tree up in its stand, I review what needs to be done. I add the tinsel branches and do my best with the lights. Without Ryan's precise input or anything suitable to stand on, the strings of bulbs are rather bunched together and when I switch them on, they remain stubbornly unlit. I also realise that I have left the baubles at home. The wind whines in the chimney and rattles at the sash windows. Looking at the angel leaning tipsily from the top branch of the tree, I discard the rest of my tea and open the Chablis instead.

This is when I notice the cupboard under the bookcase. I am intrigued by Pat's suggestion that I might find something to do in there. As I open the door, a waterfall of fir cones, dried flowers, craft paper, glitter, acrylic paints and an artist's drawing book falls onto the threadbare carpet.

I fish the Christmas CD out of the bag and put it on the CD player. The clock on the mantelpiece chimes the hour and I am surprised to see that it is now ten o'clock. This is the first evening I have spent alone in ages and I realise that despite the cold and the rain and the wonky tree, I feel peaceful in a way I haven't felt in a very long time. I turn on the electric heater and as the clear high notes of Silent Night fill the room, the tree lights flicker on. I pick up a fir cone and the silver spray paint.

The following morning, I wake to a weak light filtering through the curtains. Looking at my watch, I'm surprised to find that it is nearly ten. My morning is usually dictated by Ryan's morning routine so to lie in bed and know that the day ahead is my own, gives me a delicious thrill.

As I lean across and pull open the curtains, I gasp. The sky, yesterday a battle-ship grey, is now a clear winter blue and seems to go on for ever and in the distance is the sea view I had been promised.

Christmas Eve. The thought fills me with excitement as it did when I was a little girl. I run down the stairs two at a time to make a cup of tea to take up to bed. As I enter the living room, I see the half empty bottle of Chablis and the tree jauntily displaying its home-made decorations: silver fir cones, golden flower heads and white cut out snowflakes shimmering with glitter. It is a far cry from the white and pink baubles we bought in Selfridges. It wouldn't look out of place in a primary school but I love it.

I am replacing a cone that has fallen off the tree, when there is a knock at the door. Standing there, is a man dressed in faded jeans, ripped at the knee, and a striped rugby shirt. His blond hair is tousled by the wind and his face is tanned, despite it being winter.

'Hi. You must be Bella. Sorry I wasn't around yesterday to welcome you. I was showing some of my work at the gallery in Penlan and by the time I got back it was a bit late and I didn't want to disturb you. I also wanted to say sorry for forgetting to put on the heating. My head's like a sieve sometimes, especially when I'm in the middle of an exhibition.' He held out his hand. 'I'm Pat, by the way.'

'You're Pat? But I thought you were…'

'That I was what?'

'Oh, nothing.' I am not about to admit to this lovely stranger that I had presumed that Pat was short for Patricia. 'So, you're an artist. Are these yours?' I indicate the watercolours.

'Guilty as charged but this is some of my older work. You could come and see my new stuff in the gallery, if you like. We could take the cliff path as the weather's fine. It'll take about half an hour.' He stops suddenly and I like the way he drops his eyes. 'Sorry, I'm being silly. We've only just met and you've probably other plans.'

'No,' I say quickly. Since being with Ryan, spontaneity has not been part of my vocabulary. 'I've no other plans.'

'That's great. We can have lunch in the Mariner after, my treat.'

'Give me ten minutes to get ready. Put the kettle on, if you like.'

The coastal path is spectacular. Below us, the sea shimmers and small breakers send spray up over the rocks. Pat tells me the cottage belonged to his aunt who left it to him in her will the previous year. He had always loved the cottage and now used the rental income to help fund his flat in Penlan and his art materials.

'I also do a little teaching at the surfing school in the summer,' he says.

The exhibition is small but just as good as I expected. I marvel at the lightness in his brush strokes and the luminous quality of his water colours. I notice that one or two of the pictures have sold stickers on them.

'Do you paint?' he asks.

'I used to, but not for a long time now… Life sort of got in the way.'

We are eating sticky ribs with our fingers, having given up on knives and forks. I imagine Ryan's face and feel like a naughty child playing hooky from school.

'Well, I think that you should take the opportunity to paint while you are here. As you've seen, the view from the cottage is spectacular. There's an easel in the shed and you can use the kitchen sink to wash up in. Don't worry about making a mess – there are no more tenants until next year and I usually get a cleaning company in to get the place straight at the beginning of the season.' He stops and looks at me quizzically. 'Anyway, what brings you out here at Christmas on your own or shouldn't I ask?'

I find myself telling him about Ryan and our life together these last three years. I describe our Christmases and how in trying to keep everyone happy, we have lost our way as a couple. I feel a bit disloyal but Pat is so easy to talk to. I tell him about our final row.

'It's as if I've forgotten who I am – the Bella I used to be. Ryan means well but I sometimes feel like a child when I'm with him. I don't want to live my life to rules and timetables.'

'I see.' He makes a move as if to take my hand but then decides against it.

'Tomorrow's Christmas Day. A few friends are coming round for some food and music. It won't be anything grand but I'd like it if you would join us.'

That night, as I fall asleep, this is the last thing I think about. I have left the CD on and Silent Night is playing.

'Merry Christmas,' I say, to no one in particular.

Oddly, when I find Ryan on my doorstep on Christmas Day, I am not surprised. He has found where I am from the email confirmation on the computer. He begs me to come back home. He has put his mother off and in his hand is a brochure for Antigua.

'I've arranged everything. It's all inclusive and I've booked three excursions.' He looks around him. 'So you can leave this dump.'

I feel sorry for him, but shake my head. 'No, Ryan. I won't come with you. In fact, I've decided to rent this cottage for the rest of the week and longer if needs be.'

Ryan is aghast. 'But what about your job?'

'There are other jobs, Ryan.'

'But it's Christmas Day. You can't be on your own on Christmas Day. At least let me stay with you.'

I think about Pat and his invitation which I will not be accepting… Not this time anyway.

'Yes, I can, Ryan.'

As the car disappears down the track, I put the small turkey in the oven then climb the stairs and set the easel up at the bedroom window.

'Merry Christmas, Bella,' I say to myself.

SILENT NIGHT

Harry stretched his legs out and made himself more comfortable. He pulled his coat tighter around him and blew on his fingers.

'The trouble with Christmas,' he said, 'is that it makes you think.'

'Yes.' Ralph took off his cap and scratched his head. 'It does.'

'Any kids?'

'One.'

'These are mine. John and Amy.' He reached inside his jacket. The pictures he brought out were creased and faded. He hesitated before handing them to Ralph.

'They're beautiful. You must be very proud.'

'Too right I am. John's nearly up to here on me.' He indicated his shoulder with the side of his hand. 'They grow up in the blink of an eye. Wants to be a carpenter like his dad.'

Ralph nodded and then leaned across the worn grass. 'This is Anna. She's six.'

'Cute.' Harry said. 'And the missus?'

Ralph hesitated then brought out another photograph. A blonde-haired woman in a neat skirt and jacket smiled out sweetly. Harry saw him swallow as he looked at it before handing it to him.

'Bit of a looker that one. Bet you'll be glad to get back to her.'

Ralph turned away and stayed silent. Harry bit his tongue. Thoughtless was what he was. The last few months had made him hard.

'So she's...' Ralph stared out across the fields. Harry handed him back the photograph.

'She died last year. They tried to get word to me, but it was not easy. It was the baby, you see. She came before her time and Ida... my wife... she had always had a weak heart.'

'Sorry mate.'

'You were not to know.'

'Are the kids... ?' Harry knew that he couldn't spend another hour with this man without knowing.'

'They live with their aunt.'

Harry breathed a sigh of relief. 'Well, that's something then, isn't it?'

They were silent for a moment. 'Cigarette?'

'Thank you.'

He shook the packet and Ralph took one. 'Here.' A breeze had picked up. He cupped his hands around the match and leant over to light Ralph's cigarette before lighting his own. Around them, the red tips of other cigarettes could be seen glowing in the dark. He leaned back on his elbows and looked up at the night sky. It was a clear night, the great dome of the sky arcing above them, studded with stars.

'That's Orion.' He pointed to where three stars cut a diagonal across the black. 'There's his belt. Odd to think that other people might be looking at him too... you know in other places.' He glanced at Ralph. 'If you could be anywhere, except home of course, where would you choose?'

Ralph pulled on his cigarette, squinting as he blew out the smoke. His eyes, in the moonlight, had a faraway look.

'Forty miles from my home there are mountains. They are very beautiful, even at this time of year. The fir trees on their slopes are the deepest green and sometimes I walk the paths and listen to the silence... it is there that I would like to be.'

He stopped. A low murmuring of voices could be heard all around them.

'The Dog and Duck,' Harry said, licking his lips. 'That's where I'd go. Have a drink and a bit of a sing along. Me and the missus.'

He stood up and stamped his foot on the ground. 'Pins and needles. I get it sometimes – usually in me left. Darned nuisance when I have to sit still for a long time. When we're having to wait... you know.'

Ralph nodded and gazed into the distance. 'Yes, I know.'

'What do you do?'

'I am a doctor.'

Harry looked him up and down. 'Well I never. Didn't expect that. Not at all.'

With his cropped blond hair and his chiselled chin, Harry thought he looked more like a movie star. 'What type?'

'I am... was... a psychiatrist.'

'Well stone me! Not sure I've ever met one of them before. Don't start getting ideas about looking into me head or nothing.' He laughed. 'Not that you'd find much there.'

The corners of Ralph's mouth twitched. 'I'm sure you are wrong.'

'Funny us being here.'

'These are funny times.'

Harry shrugged. 'You can say that again, Mate.' He pointed over his shoulder at a figure huddled in his overcoat. 'Undertaker.'

Ralph raised his eyebrows. 'I would not have guessed.'

'Not much has changed for *him*.' Harry gave a grim laugh. 'And Tom there. What do you reckon he does?'

Harry watched Ralph take in the man's deep set eyes and sharp cheekbones. 'I think maybe he is the man that does the taxes.'

Harry hooted with laughter. 'Tax inspector! Hear that Tom. Ralph here thinks you're a tax inspector.'

'I did not mean to offend.'

'No offence taken eh, Tom.' The other man shook his head and took a swig from a tin cup.

'Tell me what it is he does,' Ralph said.

Harry laughed. 'He dances in shows. You know, tap and all that malarkey. Quite well known back home. Tom Boyce. Don't expect you'd have heard of him.'

Ralph shook his head. 'No, I am sorry.'

'Nothing to be sorry about.' He lowered his voice. 'Not what I'd call a real job. Wonder what's going to happen tomorrow.'

'I expect it will be as it has always been.'

'Yeh. I expect you're right... shame.'

The two men sat for a moment in silence. Harry raised the collar of his coat up around his neck and pulled his woollen scarf until it covered his chapped lips. The night had got colder and he clapped his hands together to get the circulation going.

'Chocolate?' He searched in his pocket and brought out a bar. He peeled back the wrapping and with fingers that were beginning to numb, broke off two strips. The snap was loud in the crisp air.

'Thank you.'

'What would you be doing tonight... with your children?

Ralph closed his eyes for a moment. A smile played around his lips.

'There would be a tree. So tall I would have to have a ladder to reach the top.' He breathed in the cold night air. 'I can smell the scent of the pine and from the table the sweet smell of marzipan and spice. The children they will run in from church and their faces will light up when they see the presents under the tree.'

'Mine too. Have to stop the blighters from ripping the paper off there and then. *Wait for morning* the missus is always shouting.'

'We have our presents on Christmas Eve.'

'You do?' Harry scratched his head and frowned. 'Well, fancy that. Wait there a tick.' He dropped down into the trench and searched in his kit bag. As he did, a lone voice carried on the breeze. '*Stile Nacht, heilige nacht...*'

He pulled out a pouch of tobacco, hauled himself back up and handed it to Ralph. Other voices joined the first. For a moment the two men looked at each other. 'Merry Christmas.'

Ralph placed a hand on his shoulder. '*Danke*. My friend.'

As Harry looked out over the fields of Ypres he wondered when the ceasefire would end. He clapped Ralph on the back.

'A shrink and a chippy,' he laughed, 'Who'd have thought, eh?'

A CHRISTMAS PRESENT CALLED ABBIE

The first thing I noticed was how much like her mother she looked as she stood on my doorstep, rain dripping off the ends of her hair.

'Well, go on then Abbie. Say hello to your dad.'

The girl stood expressionless and didn't make any move to come inside, despite the pouring rain. *She doesn't know how to do this anymore than I do*, I thought.

My ex-wife's sister, Lisa, gave Abbie a nudge forward. 'Go on now, Abbie. In you go. It's only until Mum's out of hospital. You'll be back home before you know it. Give me a ring, John, if there are any problems.'

She gave the little girl a kiss then turned and walked back down the drive, leaving Abbie and me looking at each other.

'Well, you'd better come in before you catch your death.' My voice sounded unnatural. I held the door open and Abbie hesitated a moment before slowly taking the handle of her Disney Princess case and pulling it over the metal door stop.

'You've grown,' I said and immediately regretted it. Wasn't that the thing that maiden aunts always said? Of course she'd grown. I counted up on my fingers – could it really have been six months since I'd seen her?

Abbie didn't seem put out. 'I'm nearly as tall as Donna Meadows in year five.'

'That's good, is it?'

'Of course,' she said and I realised that I knew nothing of her school life or her friendships.

I saw her eyes flicking across the photos of the Lamborghinis I'd taken at the car rally last summer. I'd photo-shopped them and the four prints looked like a classic Warhol, I thought.

'Why have you got cars on your wall?'

The question threw me. I wasn't sure of the answer a seven-year-old would expect. 'I like them.'

'Well, I think they're boring.'

'Oh.' We stood for a moment and the silence echoed in the hallway.

'D'you want a drink or something?' I thought about what I might have in my fridge but could only picture cans of lager. 'Milk?'

'I like Pepsi,' she said, her brows pinching.

I knew so little about this little girl – my own flesh and blood but almost a stranger to me. When my ex-wife, Donna, had phoned, out of the blue, to say she would be going into hospital for an operation and would need me to look after Abbie, my reaction had been automatic – like a knee jerk.

'Can't Lisa have her?'

'She's going away for Christmas and anyway, you're her father.'

'But she's never stayed here.' I could hear the edge of panic in my voice

'Then it's time we remedied that. It will do you good to spend more time with Abbie.' Her voice had been cool. 'You never know, you might enjoy it.'

I knew what Donna thought of me. She'd told me often enough: I was one of life's wasters, too lazy to get off my behind and get myself a proper job, living off an inheritance while playing at being a photographer, too preoccupied with my own life to see my daughter.

Indignation seethed inside me like it always did whenever I thought of Donna's accusations. Okay, so it was true that I didn't have a regular nine to five job, which sometimes meant I was late with my maintenance payment. It was also true that, had it not been for my father's death, I wouldn't have been able to pursue my ambition to be a photographer. It hurt that she thought that I didn't take my work seriously – that it was just a hobby.

I was left with one final allegation. Abbie. It was true that I hadn't seen her as much as I should have over the years but it was not because I was too busy. It was just that... I searched my heart for the reason and was shocked that the answer was as clear as day. I was scared. Scared of what she might think of me – that if she came to know me better, she might think the same as her mother.

'Where's the tree?'

I broke from my thoughts and looked at Abbie, standing in the bay window, staring out into the street. 'It should be here.' She spread her arms wide. Her stare was accusing.

'I don't have a tree.'

'Why not? It's Christmas.' Abbie folded her arms and waited for my answer.

'I suppose it's because there's no one here to see it... only me.'

'And me.'

'Yes, but I didn't know that...'

'Mum told you last week.'

I didn't know what to say. It was true. I'd had a week to prepare for Abbie's stay and what had I done? A big fat zilch. I looked around my living room and saw it through the eyes of a seven-year-old girl: big, leather settees, a chrome coffee table covered with car and photography magazines and the whole room dominated by a wall-mounted wide-screen TV. No books, no plants and definitely no cushions. The whole place screamed bachelor pad.

It was only six in the evening. What was I going to do with her? Suddenly, I wished I'd given it more thought beforehand. I searched helplessly for inspiration. 'Do you want to watch some TV... maybe a DVD?'

Abbie shrugged. 'If you like.'

I looked at the cupboard that held the DVD's and felt my neck redden. 'They might not be suitable, though.'

Abbie did not reply but pulled open the cupboard doors. I went into the kitchen and busied myself with her milk. When I came back, she was sitting in a pile of DVDs. Chaos in my ordered world.

'Look, I know they're probably not the right age for you.'

She didn't answer but picked up one and fed it into the machine.

'I don't think you should touch...'

Ignoring me, Abbie waved the controller at the screen and pressed play. As the music played, Snow White could be seen leaning over the well, *I'm wishing... I'm wishing* she sang into the green depths. Abbie lay on her tummy, her chin resting on her hands. I could hear she was singing along.

'You know this?'

'It's one of my favourites... and Dumbo... and Cinderella.'

'I have those too.'

She turned her head and looked at me, her hazel eyes so like her mother's 'Why?'

'I just have.' I said, rather too sharply.

The street was black beyond the window. I closed the curtains and thought about the evening ahead. When Darren had rung, I'd had to tell him that I wouldn't be able to meet him at The Swan as I usually did on a Friday night.

'A girl is it?'

'Something like that,' I'd said.

'Christmas Eve, then. Final of the pool tournament, or had you forgotten? Should be a good night.'

Christmas Eve. Two days time. I should be well and truly foot loose and fancy free again by then.

'You've got it, mate,' I said, ending the call.

Abbie now lay curled up on the sofa. She had taken a large pink elephant from her case and was hugging it and I thought how small she looked amongst all that leather. I wondered what she thought of being here.

'I'm hungry.'

Relieved to have something to do, I went to see what there was that would constitute a supper. In the fridge was a ready meal for one, some rather old looking Brie and the cans of beer. The cupboard didn't look any more promising: a jar of frankfurters, some tomato soup, a tin of sweet corn. I'd just have to improvise.

'Sit up straight so you don't spill it.' I handed Abbie the bowl.

'Don't we have to sit at the table. Mum says I must always sit at the table to eat.'

'And your mother's right but do you see a table?' My meals had always been taken on my lap in front of the TV. I hadn't seen the need to fork out for a dining table after the divorce.

She looked around and shook her head. I sat down next to her.

'What is it?' she asked, lifting her spoon out of the bowl and inspecting the sausage that sat in a pool of tomato soup. The sweet corn didn't do much to improve the look of it.

'It's called Dad's Surprise.'

'It's good,' Abbie said, spooning it into her mouth.

'It is?'

'Yep.' I was surprised at how much this pleased me.

'What are we going to do tomorrow?' She looked at me, the soup creating a red moustache in her upper lip. I thought of the photographs I had been planning to take of the warehouse conversions by the docks – I'd had an idea for a feature comparing the lives of their current owners with that of their nineteenth century predecessors who had worked there.

'What did you want to do?'

'Make mince pies.'

'Mince pies?'

She wiped the soup off her mouth with the back of her hand and her eyes were bright. 'Yes, it's what Mum and I do at Christmas.'

'I don't really cook,' I indicated the empty soup bowls, 'as you've just found out.'

Her face fell. 'Okay. We don't have to if you don't want to.'

'It's not that I don't want to, it's just...' I hated the way I suddenly felt. 'Look, it's fine. Mince pies it is then. Now it's probably time you were in bed.'

There was more flour on the table and the floor than there was in the bowl. It had been a task in itself to locate a mixing bowl and a baking sheet and we'd had to make a special trip to the supermarket for mincemeat.

'How many shall we make?' Abbie asked, dropping the mincemeat into each pale pastry base. 'Who's coming for Christmas?'

I was bent low, adjusting the dials on the oven. I kept my head turned away from her. I didn't really go in for Christmas much – told myself it was all a load of commercial nonsense. Anyway, now that Dad had gone, there was nobody to share it with.

'It'll just be me.' I said, my head still turned. I didn't know if she'd heard.

She had. 'Haven't you got a girlfriend?'

I shook my head.

'Why not?' She sat on the kitchen table, her little fingers pinching the edges of the pastry case together and I had a memory of her mother doing the same thing.

Since Donna, girls had come and gone but nobody had ever come close to filling the gap. I never knew them for long enough to ask them to spend Christmas day with me and anyway, I was fine on my own with my beer and an M&S turkey breast in a foil tray. It was easier that way and if I felt a little maudlin, I'd take a stroll to The Swan and meet up with some of the lads for a pint.

'We usually have Gran and Gramps and Aunty Lisa and Uncle Brian and Liam and Callum... but sometimes I wish it could just be me and Mum.'

I remembered that feeling... of wanting her all to myself. Not wanting to share. I looked at Abbie, her face dusted in flour, and for the first time wondered whether I had been jealous of her. I shook the thought away.

'Well, these certainly look good,' I said, taking the first tray out of the oven. 'There probably won't be any left by Christmas anyway.'

Abbie dusted off her hands. 'And now we'll make some paper chains.'

'We will? What with.'

'Mum usually buys the gummy strips from the newsagents but we can cut some out.'

I looked around. 'Out of what?'

'Those boring magazines you have lying around... the ones with the pictures of cars and buildings. We can use those.'

'We can?'

'Yes, it's easy and we'll put glitter on them. Mummy put some in my case. Of course we have to have Christmas music when we're making them... it's the law.'

I couldn't help laughing. 'I'm not sure I've got any.'

'Well, lucky I put a CD in my case then. Mum told me to.'

The light was fading and the floor was covered in strips of paper. We had made some glue out of flour and water and Frank Sinatra was telling us to have ourselves a merry little Christmas. I was so absorbed in the cutting that the ringing of my mobile made me jump.

My heart gave a little lurch as it always did when I heard Donna's voice, even after all this time. 'It's your mum, Abbie. She wants to speak to you.'

Abbie grabbed the phone and her little face was serious. 'Yes, of course I'm alright with Dad.' There was a pause. 'No, he didn't get a babysitter... he's been right here with me. We had Chinese for dinner and then ice cream with sprinkles on it. Will you be coming home soon, Mummy?'

I was surprised when Abbie held out the phone to me. 'Mum wants to talk to you.'

There was a hint of uncertainty in Donna's voice. I listened to what she had to tell me, all the while watching Abbie fold and stick the paper chains – her little hands shiny with glue.

'So they can't tell you when they're going to let you go home?' I said, stunned at the news. 'What, keep her for the whole of Christmas? No, No I'm sorry... of course I'm okay with that. No, it won't be spoiling any plans. I'll hand you back to Abbie.'

So Abbie was staying for Christmas. My heart beat faster, from fear or excitement, I had no idea which. I was just getting used to this thought when another entered my head. Donna had chosen *me* to look after her. Not her own mother and father. Not her sister, who would have cut short her holiday if asked... but *me*.

'Will you read me a story, Dad?' Abbie stood beside the bed in her Aladdin pyjamas. The pink elephant was under her arm.

'I don't think you'd like Lord of the Rings, Abbie.'

'I don't mean one of your books. I mean one from there.'

She pointed to the wardrobe and I knew what she was talking about. I saw again my twenty-three year old self stopping outside the bookshop, mesmerised by the display of children's books in the window. Something had drawn me inside and when I came out again, I had a complete set of Disney stories in a plastic bag that bounced heavily against my leg.

I leant into the wardrobe and brought out the box of books, placing them on the end of the bed.

'Who were these books for, Dad?' Abbie asked, turning each page in delight. 'And the DVDs... who did you buy them for?'

I looked at my hands and my voice, when it came out, was barely a whisper. 'They were for you, Abbie. I bought them for you.'

Abbie had been asleep for an hour. The sitting room was strung with garlands of paper chains and we had made some paper snowflakes out of my printer paper and stuck them on the windows. She's right, I thought, we do need a tree... and a turkey... and a Christmas pudding and crackers to pull. For the first time in years, I was getting excited about the prospect.

I poured myself a glass of wine and took the second CD out of its case and put it in the player. The jingle of sleigh bells filled the room, reminding me of something else I would be needing to do – I had forgotten all about Santa.

Come on it's lovely weather for a sleigh ride together with you... that first Christmas, in our little two up, two down, Donna and I had sung along to the radio as we sat, back to back, wrapping each other's gifts. I had thought that it would last for ever. Us I mean. And when Abbie had come along, I had thought her perfect and promised myself that I would be the best father in the world. But it hadn't happened that way. By the time she was a year old, the cracks had already started to appear in our marriage.

I put my glass on the coffee table and opened the sideboard cupboard. The album was heavy, covered in a shiny, plastic sleeve. Sitting back down, I turned the pages. There were photos of our wedding, the wind blowing Donna's veil across her face outside the registry office. Other pictures showed us together on a beach somewhere – I remembered setting the timer on the camera and placing it on a gatepost before running back to stand with my arm around my wife. Then there was Donna, smiling at the camera, one hand resting on her rounded belly.

The large envelope tucked into the back of the album contained several large photographs. I knew them well – had looked at them time and again over the years: black and white prints of Abbie. The photographer had captured the essence of the sleeping baby, had caught the dappled pattern of the leaves on her pale face as she'd lain beneath the tree and the delicate trace of veins on her translucent eyelids.

'I can't sleep, Daddy.'

Abbie leant against the doorpost. One hand held the trunk of her pink elephant, the thumb of the other had found its way into her mouth. I held out my hand to her. 'Come and sit with me.'

She climbed onto the settee and snuggled against me. 'Who's that?'

'It's you, Abbie. When you were very small.'

She traced a finger over the baby's face, her fine hair and rosebud lips parted in sleep.

'Whoever took this picture loved me very much,' she said.

I looked at my daughter, and wondered at the years I had missed. The first steps, the first day at school and all the little thing in between. The truth was, I had been too young back then, unable to adapt to the changes. Unable to share. But there was one undeniable truth.

This Christmas had given me a second chance, a chance to prove to Donna and to Abbie, that I had changed.

'Yes,' I said, stroking the hair back from her forehead. 'He did.'

DO YOU BELIEVE IN ANGELS

'Do you believe in angels, Granddad?'

The old man puts another log on the fire and grunts. ''Course not. Whoever put such silly ideas into your head, child?'

The girl glances at her grandmother, whose head is bent over her darning, but says nothing – not wanting to get her into trouble. She won't tell him that every night, when the gas lamp has been turned down and the curtains drawn at her little window, her grandmother will take the silver-handled brush from the dresser and brush her golden hair until it fans out around her pillow. Nor will she mention the stories the old lady tells as she draws the bristles through her hair.

'There was once a girl with skin as white as an angel's. She had many brothers and sisters but she was lonely...'

The girl looks around her. She is lonely sometimes, too, with just her grandparents for company. Since her mother was taken from them, this small cottage at the wood's edge has become her home and she can barely remember the paved streets and terraces of before. At first, her father slept on the couch by the fire but now he is away fighting in the trenches, so her grandfather says.

A Christmas tree stands in the corner of the room – she has helped her grandmother to decorate it. She looks up. Where there should be an angel, there is only a branch of pointed fir. Her grandfather will not allow an angel.

In the window of the haberdashers in town, there is a tree – she saw it when she went with her grandmother to collect groceries. She'd pressed her nose against the glass and wished that she could lift the angel, with the white wings, from the top of its glittering branches and take it home with her. Instead, she had turned away, imagining her grandfather's voice in her head; hearing his gruff tones as he told her that all the angels were needed to look after the young men on the battlefields.

'When will father come?' she asks.

Her grandfather's eyes narrow and her grandmother touches a finger to her lips. 'Hush child,' she says, drawing her close so that the brooch at her throat presses against her cheek. 'Hush.'

That night, when the moon has risen above the fir trees beyond her window, her grandmother settles on the end of the counterpane of her little bed. The springs squeak as she sits.

'Shall I tell you more?'

Nodding, the girl closes her eyes and lets her grandmother's words fill the room, where shadows play in the light of the gas lamp.

'The girl with the skin as white as an angel's grew up and many men looked her way but she was waiting... waiting until the right man would hold his hand out to her. Not any man, mind you, but someone with a heart so full of joy that he would be able to share it.'

On the shelf above her bed is the book that tells of men with wings as white as a swan's and a girl as small as your thumb. Most magical of all, though, is the story her grandmother tells – the one she wants to hear.

'One day,' the old woman continues, her voice as gentle as the firs that stir in the wind outside her window, 'the girl left the city and went to work as a maid in a beautiful house, surrounded by lawns and a wide, blue lake.'

The young girl closes her eyes. She sees the house in her mind and in her dreams – it's arched windows and mellow stone walls.

'Did she like it there, Grandma?' she asks, although she knows the answer.

'Oh yes, child, though the work was hard and the days very long.'

The girl touches a hand to the old woman's white skin, tracing the blue veins in the soft light. 'Tell me about the boy...'

She feels the touch of her grandmother's lips on her forehead, her breath soft against her skin.

'Tomorrow,' she says. 'I will tell you tomorrow.'

Her grandfather stands by the window, his weathered hands clasped behind his back. Each day, he stands and looks and the girl wonders what he is seeing.

'Sometimes, I think I hear angels, Granddad. When I am collecting firewood for the stove. Do you hear them?'

He turns his blue eyes to her and she clasps her hands to her chest, wondering what his answer will be. Does he hear them too as he fells the trees with his axe, leaving them for the men from the sawmill to drag onto their carts?

His jaw is tight. 'I hear nothing but the wind, child. No more of your silly questions, now.'

'Come,' her grandmother takes her by the hand and leads her into the scullery. 'Let your grandfather be. You can see his back is aching and there are sheets to be folded.'

As she reaches the door, she turns her head and sees that her grandfather has turned back to the window, his forehead resting on the glass and his breath a mist on the pane.

'Why is granddad so sad?'

Her grandmother bends to the laundry basket and if she has heard, she does not say so. Instead, she continues with her story.

'The young man's face was full of smiles as he stood at the door of the beautiful house with its lawns fanning out around it. As he stood there, with his hands in his pockets, waiting for the gardener to give him his orders, something in his easy manner and smiling blue eyes touched the girl's heart.'

'Did she love him?' The girl's heart thrills at the question.

Her grandmother hands her a pillow slip. 'Of course, she did. How could she not?'

Satisfied, she continues to fold and smooth, noticing how her grandmother's hands are swift and practiced. As they carry the pile of bed linen up the wooden stairs, the bells and glass baubles on the tree shiver in the draft that creeps under the back door. Passing above it, she wants to reach out a hand and touch the place where the angel should sit, but her arms are full.

'Do you think father will be lonely?' It is almost Christmas and outside her bedroom window the night sky hides every star like a secret.

'There are others there with him, child... other fathers with hearts filled with thoughts of their home and their children.'

She turns her face to the pillow. 'I wish he was here.'

Her grandmother shifts her weight and is silent for a moment and the girl knows that her thoughts are far away in France. Downstairs, they can hear the soft tread of her grandfather's boots on the flagstones, pacing an endless journey across the room.

'We all do,' the old woman says.

'Tell me more about the boy with the smiling eyes.' Her grandmother's words can comfort her as well as any arms.

Although her eyelids have closed, she hears the smile in the old woman's voice.

'It was Christmas Eve and the girl had been sent to market, a basket on her arm. Have I told you how the snowflakes had fallen that night, as silent as an angel's wing? Well, as she stepped outside the house, she saw that the lawns now wore a glittering white mantle.'

The girl clasps her hands around her knees, her eyes wide. 'It sounds so beautiful.'

The old woman nods. 'It was.'

'But what of the boy?'

Her grandmother sighs. 'When the snowball hit the tree beside her, a shower of snow fell from its branches... like the most beautiful waterfall.'

The girl claps her hands. 'And he laughed and said he had something to show her.'

A tut escapes the old woman's lips. 'Not so fast, child. Whose story is it to tell? The boy was standing on the terrace, snow on his gloved hands and laughter in his eyes. At first the girl thought to scold him but there was something in the way he stood, so tall and fine, that made her blush instead.'

A gust of wind rattles the casement and the girl pulls the quilt up around her shoulders. Downstairs, she can hear her grandfather poking at the fire and cursing the embers that spit onto the floor. She wishes she could make him smile but knows that while her father is away, her attempts will be brushed aside like the ash in the grate.

Her grandmother reaches out and smoothes a curl from her forehead, distracted by the sound of the latch on the back door. 'Shall I tell you more?' she asks.

'Tell me about the garden.'

'The boy took the young maid's hand and led her onto the lawn. He stood a moment, letting the snow drift onto his cheeks, his hair... and then, as she watched, he fell back onto the white snow.'

The girl laughs. She loves this part the best. 'Did the mistress not see?'

'They were in the morning room on the other side of the house, taking breakfast, although the girl did glance at the blank windows to be sure.'

'And then...'

'And then, laughing, she threw herself back too and the snow received her like a heavenly cloud. For a moment they lay there, side by side on the white lawns, snow falling softly onto their faces.'

The footfall on the stairs is so quiet, neither hear it.

'Go on,' the girl urges.

Her grandmother closes her eyes, and there are tears on her cheeks.

'Then a great happiness came over her and she raised her arms in an ark above her head and back down, leaving an imprint in the snow... like wings. With shining eyes, the boy took her hand and helped her to her feet and together, hand in hand, they walked away. Before they reached the iron gate, he turned and looked at the pattern she had made in the snow and do you know what he said?'

Her grandfather stands in the doorway. He looks at his wife and his granddaughter and his eyes are tender. In his hand is a letter, he caresses it with his thumb. She recognises her father's handwriting.

When he speaks, his voice is gruff but there is the smile of the boy in his eyes.

'He told her she was an angel,' he says. 'How did I forget?'

.

A SONG FOR CHRISTMAS

I looked at Hattie in amazement. She had just told me to grow up and I have to admit I had taken it hard.

'It's not that I don't love you, Cal. It's just that I'm not sure that you're good for me... or for Ben.'

Wracking my brains for something intelligent to say, to stop her from carrying on, instead I found myself doing my impression of Donald Duck. It's something I've been able to do since I was a boy – forcing air into the space between my cheek and my jaw and then pushing it out through the side of my mouth.

'Oh boy, oh boy, oh boy...'

'It's not funny, Cal. This is exactly what I'm talking about. Everything's a joke with you.'

I studied her face: the clear grey eyes under her frown, the beautiful lips pressed together, and with a lurch, realised that I was in danger of losing it all.

'Hattie, I...'

'Look. I know that things are going well for the band at the moment and I'm pleased for you, I really am. But I just don't think I'm ready for all this. I need to feel settled, for Ben's sake, and you and Chris just seem to wind each other up. You're like a couple of adolescents sometimes.'

Chris was the drummer of *Boyz inc* and my best buddy in all the world. We'd started the band together after we'd left school and as far as I could remember, had never fallen out. Okay, so we liked to have a laugh and still found *American Pie* funny but it was unfair for Hattie to say that next door's Labrador was more mature than me.

'What I can't understand,' she said now, standing in the doorway of the living room, her hands folded around her middle, 'is how you manage to write such beautiful lyrics to your songs but when it comes to us, to our relationship, you revert to schoolboy humour. That's your problem, Cal. You think life's just a big joke.'

'I don't, Hat. It's just...'

But I had to stop there because, if I was honest, I couldn't think of a good answer. When I wrote my songs, a picture of Hattie was always in my head – her smile, the way her fair hair fell about her face, her lips. I wrote those songs for her, only I was too damn pig-headed to tell her... and if I did, I knew she would never believe me.

'Mum, I'm hot.' Ben pressed himself against Hattie's side, his little arms wound tightly round her leg.

Hattie bent down and felt his forehead with the back of her hand. 'You do feel a bit hot, sweetie.

Snuggle down on the settee and we'll watch some TV together.'

'I can't find Dinky Dino.'

'He's probably still in your bed. I'll find him in a minute. Now say goodbye to Callum.'

Ben buried his head in Hattie's skirt – he was a sweet little boy but we were still at that 'getting to know you' stage. I did know how much he loved his dinosaur though, with it's long neck and huge green spots. For a fleeting moment I thought about helping him to look for it but Hattie was already ushering me to the front door.

'You're on your Christmas tour in a few days, Cal. Let's use this time apart to think about what we really want. I do love you, but I've got to think of what's best for Ben. He needs a father figure... not a big brother.'

I looked into her beautiful grey eyes and realised that she meant every word. There was a sinking feeling inside me. Maybe she was right: I was the clown of the band – the papers were full of my silly escapades with Chris or mug shots of me gurning at the lens. It was all good publicity for the tour but now I could see that maybe it was incompatible with my relationship with Hattie.

As I walked down the front path to my car, checking first that there were no paparazzi about, Hattie called after me.

'I mean it, Cal. Think what it is you want.'

I shut the door and leant my back against it, trying to fight the wave of sadness that threatened to envelop me.

From the living room, I heard Ben call out, 'Mum, I want Dinky Dino.'

Closing my eyes for a second, I took a deep breath – it was stupid to feel this way. It had to be for the best. After all, I couldn't have let our relationship drift on as it was, without knowing how Callum felt about me... about us. Whenever I tried to bring up the subject, he would just make a joke or sing a line from a cheesy song in the voice of some cartoon character or other. In fact, the last time I had tried to talk about my feelings, he'd held up an imaginary microphone and in his best Tina Turner voice, warbled: *What's love got to do, got to do with it...* No, it was clear that Ben and I would be better off without him.

'Look, here he is.' A search of Ben's room had resulted in Dino being released from a tangle of bed sheets. I put the soft toy on the settee next to him and studied his face. He was flushed and his fringe was sticking to his damp forehead. I touched his skin again with the back of my hand.

'You feel very hot, Ben. You must be coming down with a cold – I'll find you some Calpol.'

He looked up at me and his eyes seemed shinier than usual. 'Is Callum here?'

'No, darling, you saw him go. He has to get ready for his Christmas show – remember I told you about it?'

'You said that there'd be lots of lights and lots of people there... all screaming.'

This of course was true, although I hadn't remembered putting it quite like that. When I was with Callum, it was hard to believe that my boyfriend's face adorned the walls of thousands of young girls. I smiled to myself. That was what I liked most about him: he was so down to earth – anyone meeting him for the first time would think him just an ordinary guy rather than one who had a hit single in the top 10 charts.

When I'd first met him in my local, I'd mistaken him for a waiter. 'Do you know if the scampi comes with tartar sauce?' I'd asked as he'd walked by.

He'd stopped and given a lopsided grin. 'I don't know. You hum it and I'll sing it.'

It had taken me a moment to realise my mistake, but my apologies had been brushed off. 'Hey, it's cool. I've been mistaken for worse.'

As my friend Lisa and I finished our meal, Callum picked up a guitar from where it leant against the wall and, sitting on a stool in the corner, started to sing. It was an acoustic rendition of *You, Me, Us* and it was beautiful.

'He sounds just like the singer from *Boys inc,'* I'd whispered to Lisa. 'What a great cover version.'

'Looks a bit like him as well,' she'd replied but I wouldn't have known – I'd only heard them on the radio. I was mesmerised by his voice though.

As we stood up to leave, he caught my eye and smiled.

'Going so soon,' he asked with mock concern. 'I wasn't that bad, was I?'

'Not at all. I think your set was great. Your voice is just like Callum Dale's.'

He lowered his voice to a whisper. 'That's because I *am* Callum Dale. I've rented a property just outside the town. Thought it might be a bit more private down here.'

I tried to stop my jaw from dropping. 'Goodness.'

'Don't look so shocked. I've only just moved here and this is my way of ingratiating myself with the locals. I wasn't sure how they'd take to a boy band member and his entourage intruding on their rural idyll – though I'm not sure many of them have heard of *Boys inc.*'

I laughed, looking at the handful of middle aged couples enjoying their meals. It seemed I wasn't the only one not to have recognised him. 'I think you're right there.'

'Well,' Callum said, resting his chin on the end of his guitar case. 'I hope I'll see you again. The house has got a recording studio and the lads are coming down from the smoke to try some stuff for the new album – I should be around for the next few months at least while we thrash it out, and it will be nice to be able to tell them the locals are friendly.'

I'd tried to stop my heart from beating so quickly... the way he'd looked at me with his playful brown eyes had done strange things to my stomach.

'That would be nice,' was all I could manage.

That was seven months ago now and it was hard to believe that things had progressed so quickly but there was something in Callum's boyish charm that had won me over and we were soon seeing each other several times a week, whenever I could get a babysitter for Ben. A month ago, I had been surprised and relieved when he had asked to meet my son, saying that he would have asked sooner but hadn't wanted to push it.

But I wouldn't think of that. Now it would be just Ben and Me. I went and sat on the settee next to him.

'Mummy, it hurts here.' His little arm was thrown across his forehead.

Pulling back the collar of his pyjamas, my heart clenched as I saw dark spots beneath his pale skin. Fear gripping me, I rushed to the kitchen and grabbed a glass off the shelf. I knelt beside Ben and pressed it gently against his skin as I'd seen them do on TV. The spots were still clear to see.

'Please, God. No!'

Grabbing my car keys from the coffee table, I scooped my son up in my arms. 'It's alright, darling. We're just taking a little trip to the hospital.'

Chris did a drum roll that was so loud I jumped.

'What's up?' he said. 'You've looked like a wet weekend... all wet weekend.'

I strummed my fingers across the strings of my guitar and stared out of the window at the rain that continued to fall from the December sky. The fields outside my house were as grey as my mood.

'Nothing's up.'

'Could have fooled me, Mate. Do me a favour and snap out of it before the tour starts,' Chris said, tapping the drumsticks against his arm. 'Nobody likes a misery guts – especially not our fans. Just think, in a week's time we'll be in Copenhagen.'

I tried to think about what he was saying but the only picture I had in my head was of a girl with grey eyes, her pale hair falling across her face.

'Come on, Callum. We need to lighten the mood. Arm wrestle? Bubble gum blowing competition? Pin the tail on the sound recordist?'

I tried to smile but my heart wasn't in it. Outside, the wind was bending the trunks of the birches and I wondered what Hattie and Ben were doing. When I turned back to the room, Chris was beside me, my mobile phone in his hand.

'For goodness sake, just ring her,' he said, shoving it into my hand. 'I can't stand to look at your miserable face a minute longer.'

I tried her mobile first and then, when there was no answer, tried her home phone. It rang for several minutes and in that time, I thought of all the things I could say to her. 'Life has no meaning without you... I'll try harder this time...' but somehow everything sounded like some horrible cliché.

I was just about to put the phone down when I heard a voice on the other end.

'Hattie, thank goodness...'

'It's not Hattie, Callum – it's me, Jane.'

I had met Hattie's mother a few times and we'd always got on well. 'Is Hattie there? Can I speak to her?'

There was a pause on the other end of the phone. 'You obviously haven't heard, Callum. Hattie's taken Ben to hospital, they think he may have meningitis.'

Suddenly, the room felt very cold. 'Is he alright?'

'They don't know yet. They're doing tests. I've just popped in to collect some clothes for my daughter.'

I sank down onto the chair. 'Thank you... thank you for telling me.'

'I'm surprised you didn't know.' Her voice sounded concerned. 'Is everything all right between you two?'

'I don't know, Jane,' I said, and realised as I said it, how much the truth hurt. 'I really don't know.'

The ward was strung with paper chains and someone had scrawled Happy Christmas across the white board above the nurses' station. Someone had made an effort to make the children's ward as homely as possible but as the nurse took Ben's temperature, the reindeer ears on her head seemed out of place against the white walls and strip lighting.

'He's responding well to the antibiotics, Miss Peterson. He should be home in a week or so.'

Ben looked so small in the bed and my heart clenched when I thought of what might have been. He was asleep now and the rash was just a pale reminder of how ill he had been. Cards and presents covered his bedside table but when he had last woken, it was Dinky Dino he had asked for – something I had forgotten to ask Mum to bring when she'd gone to the house to collect my things. I couldn't expect her to go back again.

Despite the noise of the ward, I felt suddenly alone and, with a jolt, I realised that it was Callum that I wanted with me – making me laugh and telling me that it would be all right. But Callum was in Copenhagen, on the first leg of his tour, and after what I'd said to him the previous week, I wouldn't be surprised if he'd forgotten me already. There would, after all, be plenty of girls who would give their right arm to take my place.

I looked around the ward. Most of the other children were awake, playing with toys or watching TV on their ipads. The parents who were there were chatting to each other, putting on brave faces and discussing whether their child might be well enough to go home for Christmas.

'I think I might pop home and get Ben's dinosaur,' I said to the nurse as she wrote on his chart. 'Then he'll have it here when he wakes up.'

'Good idea – you've hardly left his bedside since he came in. He'll be asleep for a while and we'll let you know straight away if there are any changes.'

Kissing Ben's forehead and trying not to look at the drip in his little arm, I picked up my bag and left the ward. I would be back before he woke.

'I'm afraid we can't let you see him unless you are a relative.'

The nurse with the red antlers on her head stared at me as if she'd seen me somewhere before. I put down my guitar case and glanced past the nurses station to where Ben lay in his bed. He looked smaller than I remembered him and the sight of the tube in his arm made me wince.

Harriet wasn't with him, which I took to be a good sign, but for some inexplicable reason, I knew in my heart that I couldn't leave until I had seen for myself that he was okay. The boys hadn't been happy, and I thought that my manager was going to burst a blood vessel, when I'd told them that I was taking the first flight home. It had taken that first concert to realise that all the success in the world meant nothing to me if Harriet wasn't there to share it, and the only place I had wanted to be was by her side. The thought of her suffering was more than I could bear... but what if she didn't want me here?

I heard whispering behind me. 'It's Callum Dale. I'm sure it is.'

As I saw the two nurses point to my guitar case I had an idea.

'I've come to entertain the children,' I said, whipping off my beanie hat. A couple of the mother's gasped. 'I have a Christmas song I thought they'd like to hear.'

The nurse with the reindeer antlers smiled and blushed. 'Mr Dale! I am so sorry I didn't recognise you. Please do come in and meet everyone.'

As I walked into the ward, I was aware of twelve pairs of eyes on me and I felt more nervous than I had done before the last concert. As I passed Ben's bed, he sat up and smiled at me.

'Callum, you're here!'

'You bet, Mate. Nothing would have stopped me.'

I pulled out a chair from beside one of the beds and sat down on it, taking my guitar out of my case. 'This song,' I said, looking at the little boy with the grey eyes just like his mother's, 'is called Dinky Dino Hates Christmas.'

I strummed the first chord slowly and put on my gravest voice as I began '*Have you met my pet called Dinky... his covered in spots and his feet are stinky...*'

From his bed, Ben gave a chuckle that warmed my heart. I winked at him and carried on. '*With a belch he'd whisper pardon me as he ate the balls from the Christmas tree!*'

The children, either side of me, clapped their hands and looked at their mothers to see if they were shocked but they were smiling and swaying to the rhythm of the song and in the doorway a huddle of nurses were giggling.

I was so engrossed in the song, that I didn't notice Hattie until she was beside Ben's bed. She held Dinky Dino out to him and the little boy took the stuffed dinosaur and danced him across his sheets in time with the music.

As I came to the end of the song, the ward erupted in applause and I bowed and put on my best Donald Duck voice. 'Oh boy, oh boy, oh boy!'

But there were only two people in that room I wanted to please.

I looked at Harriet, sitting so still on Ben's bed and all of a sudden I felt shy. 'I'm not sure it'll get to number one.'

'You came back, Cal?'

For once I was serious. 'You and Ben needed me.'

She said nothing for a moment and then I felt her hand in mine. 'What I said to you the other day, when I said Ben needed a father not a brother, well, I was wrong. What Ben needs is someone warm and funny who cares for us... someone like you, Callum.'

'Really?'

She put a hand up to my cheek. 'You wrote that song for Ben. What could be more caring than that?'

For a moment I thought about pulling the curtains around the bed to give us some privacy and then thought, what the heck, I wanted the whole world to know.

'I never told you, Harriet... but you know that song on my album, *Love you till the end of time*.'

She looked at me with the grey eyes I loved so much and nodded and I knew it was time to tell her.

'Well.' I put Harriet's hand to my lips and kissed it. 'I wrote it for you.'

THE MEMORY PURSE

Tracy placed the box on the table next to the water dispenser in the homeowners' club lounge. She'd wrapped it that morning in holly-covered Christmas paper and curled the ends of the shiny ribbon, that secured it, with the blunt end of her scissors. She'd only just got the job at The Cedars Retirement Village and was keen to impress.

'This,' she said, smiling at the residents, 'is where you can put your suggestions for our Christmas outing. Something that we can all do together.'

'Please, not the pantomime again.' Gloria Eastwood put down her hand of cards, eying Tracy from under her thick grey fringe. 'Last year, Aladdin forgot his lines and the genie got stuck in the lamp. I don't think my heart will take another evening like that.'

'Which is exactly why I've put this box here, Gloria. So that you can let me know what you'd like to do.'

She glanced at the closed door next to the reception. *Manager* was written on a name plate on the front of it.

'To be honest, if we don't get any good ideas, Mrs Derbyshire will make the decision for you and it might not be what you want.'

It was obvious that Mrs Derbyshire was efficient and took pride in overseeing the complex of twenty-four retirement flats but, from what Tracy had heard, she was not known for her imagination or spontaneity. It was nice that the residents' health and safety was uppermost in her mind but it wouldn't make for an exciting trip.

'What about you, Mr Bhadu? I'm sure there's something you'd like to do.'

'Why are you asking him, Tracy?' Gloria waved a six of clubs at the elderly gentleman in a white turban who stood by the window, looking out onto the communal garden. It was a pleasant space and was popular in the summer. 'He's Sikh, aren't you, dear.'

Tracy felt herself colour. 'Oh, how stupid of me. I'm so sorry. I wasn't thinking.'

Mr Bhadu turned from the window and smiled kindly at her. 'Gloria is right. Sikhism is my religion but just because I do not celebrate Christmas as you do, does not mean that I do not enjoy an outing. Parveen Masood is Muslim and Jack Larson doesn't believe in anything at all, as far as I know, but I'm sure they'd agree with me.'

Tracy clapped her hands. 'I'm so pleased. We'll call it a winter outing instead – that way everyone can make a suggestion.' She turned to the box and placed her hand on top of it. 'Just put your ideas in this slot and next week I'll have a look through them and have a chat with Mrs Derbyshire.'

'Good luck with that, dear,' Gloria said, taking two cards from the pile in front of her. She shielded them with her hand so that the two ladies who sat opposite her couldn't see. 'I bought my flat at The Cedars in 2010, the year the flats were built, so Margery Derbyshire and I go back a long way. Despite your cunning plan, it'll be the pantomime as always, bless her. You mark my words.'

'Have you lived here all your life, Mr Bhadu?'

Tracy unplugged the vacuum cleaner and started to wind up the cable. Her job as assistant manager at The cedars required her to housekeep for any of the homeowners who requested it.

'What was that, my dear?'

Mr Bhadu's flat was on the ground floor. He'd hung a birdfeeder from a hook on the wall outside his window and was watching a small yellow bird, with a red face, peck at the nuts.

'I was just asking whether you'd always lived here… in England I mean.'

'I came here as a young man in 1962.' He watched as the bird flew away, to be replaced by another. 'That one is a goldfinch, you know. Many migrate to Spain in the winter but not this one it seems.'

'I can't imagine what it must have been like living in India. I haven't been to very many places myself. Only the Isle of Wight and Tenerife.'

Mr Bhadu's face took on a faraway look. 'India was very different to England, my dear. When I was young, growing up in the Punjab, there was no television and we didn't have a car. We walked everywhere or cycled. Except for my father who rode a Vespa – he'd let me ride on the back of it sometimes.'

'That sounds like fun.'

'It was. I have good memories. My brothers and I, we would sleep on the terrace when it was hot and when we were not at school we looked after the goats or played marbles. My favourite game was cricket though.'

'My dad plays in the summer and my mum helps with the teas. She's draws the line at making cakes though. Says they can have biscuits from the Co-op or lump it.'

Mr Bhadu smiled. 'My mother did all the cooking on a kerosene stove but everything she made us was delicious.'

Tracy joined him at the window. 'Why did you come to England?'

Mr Bhadu fingered the woven purse he always wore around his neck. 'I was twenty-three and wanted to make a better life for myself and for my wife, Neeta. My cousin had gone before me – he used to send home books for us children to read. My favourite was the one about a snowman who came to life. I'd never seen a snowman. I'd never seen snow.'

Tracy thought of the break times at her school when they'd spilled out onto the playground for snowball fights. It probably wouldn't be allowed now. Too dangerous.

'I had seen an advertisement for workers from the commonwealth to come over,' Mr Bhadu continued. 'In India I had trained to be an engineer – I thought it would be the right thing to do.'

'It must have been strange. Leaving your family and everything.'

'It was, but my greatest sadness was leaving my wife, Neeta,' he said, rubbing a hand down his face. 'We had only been married six months. There is a picture of her there on the sideboard.'

Tracy had seen the photograph before when she'd been vacuuming the room. Mr Bhadu's wife was sitting at a sewing machine, her shiny black hair pulled back from her face and a half smile on her lips. She picked it up and studied it.

'She's beautiful.'

'Oh, yes. Most certainly. Come sit by me and I'll tell you a little about her.' Putting down his stick, he sat down on the settee by the window.

Tracy smiled and joined him. 'I'd like that.'

'My wife did not have a formal education but she was quick and nimble with her fingers. She made this for me as a gift when I went to England.'

He lifted the embroidered purse so that Tracy could see it better. 'She told me that it was where I should keep all my memories of India so I wouldn't forget. That wasn't all though. She said in time the purse would fill with new memories made in my new country and that only when each had equal weight would I be truly happy. Here feel it.'

Tracy lifted the purse on its string but it was as light as a feather. There was nothing in it.

Mr Bhadu registered the question in her eyes. 'You think the purse is empty but you forget, they are my memories in here, not yours. To me, the purse is almost full.'

Tracy touched a finger to Neeta's gentle face. 'Did your wife ever come over here?'

He shook his head and took the photograph from her. 'Sadly, my wife passed away of typhoid fever before I could send for her. There is not a day goes by that I do not think of her though.'

'I'm so sorry Mr Bhadu.'

'You do not need to be, for the small time we had together in India is in here. It is with me always.'

He lifted the embroidered purse to his lips and kissed it and, from the smile on his lips, Tracy knew that it was true.

'That's a lovely story. Thank you for telling me.'

Mr Bhadu patted Tracy's hand with his own darker one. 'You are welcome, my dear. Now please forgive me for keeping you from your work. I know how busy you are. You don't want to be sitting here with me regaling you with stories of my youth.'

Tracy looked at the photograph of Neeta and smiled. 'That's where you're wrong, Mr Bhadu. Hearing everyone's stories is what makes it so interesting working here.'

'That is a good thing.' Getting up, he went back to his position at the window. 'We are lucky to have you.'

Tracy got up to go but stopped as she reached the door. 'Oh, Mr Bhadu, I nearly forgot to ask you. Have you put your idea for a winter outing into the box yet?'

The elderly man had his back to her, his white kurta-pyjamas crumpled from where he'd been sitting. He was watching a robin hop along the fence that separated his flat from the next.

'No, dear. I am happy to let others choose. I am aware that there is little room left in my purse for new memories but I'm sure I will enjoy the outing just the same.'

It was the end of the week and Tracy's suggestion box was empty, the pieces of paper lying in a pile on the club lounge table. She picked one at random.

'Vintage dance at the Community Centre. I like that one, Gloria. Good choice.' She took out another. 'A day at the races. That's Jack's idea. Well, we've got Mallory Park Circuit forty minutes away. It's an idea.'

'I don't like motor racing,' Gloria said, folding her arms.

Jack shrugged his shoulders. 'Well, I don't like dancing.'

As Tracy read out the other ideas, it was clear it was going to be difficult to find something that everyone wanted to do. Parveen didn't like opera and Gloria's card partners didn't want lunch at the garden centre.

Mrs Derbyshire had been listening to all this from the doorway of her office. 'Well, ladies and gentlemen. I think that in the absence of any decision being made, I shall make it for us all. The pantomime it is. I believe it's Jack and the Beanstalk this year.'

Gloria groaned. 'And you can guarantee the backside of the cow will fall off the stage like it did three years ago.'

Tracy was about to speak but Mrs Derbyshire shook her head. 'It was a nice idea, Tracy, but I could have told you it wouldn't work. You'll enjoy the pantomime.'

Picking up the pieces of paper, Tracy returned them to the box and shut the lid. She felt deflated.

She'd been so sure that there would be something that everyone would agree on.

'Do not be disheartened, child.'

Mr Bhadu was standing at the large sliding doors of the communal lounge, watching a tiny thrush with orange flashes on its sides. It was pecking at the berries in the hedge. 'That's a redwing. It's come all the way here from Iceland. It's appearance in the garden is a sure sign that it will be a cold winter.'

Tracy joined him and stared out at the grey sky and the sodden grass. 'It certainly brightens up the garden. Why do you think it was so difficult to find something we all wanted to do?'

Mr Bhadu smiled at her kindly, his dark eyes willing her to understand. He touched the purse around his neck with his finger. 'Everyone is different. We all have our own stories, our own memories and our own pleasures. Just like the birds in the garden, it would be a dull place if we were all the same.'

'I suppose you're right.' She looked at the clock. 'I'd better get the tea urn on but, before I do, you never finished telling me your story. How come you stayed in England after your wife died? Didn't you miss India?'

'Of course I did but I stayed here because I knew it was what Neeta would have wanted me to do. We had planned it together and my purse had only a few memories of England in it.'

'And your wife said you needed to have an equal weight of memories from both countries to be truly happy.'

Mr Bhadu nodded. 'You are a good listener. You remember it well.'

'That's because it interests me.'

'It was hard at first,' Mr Bhadu continued. 'I thought, with my qualification, that I would get skilled work but all I was offered was a job at the foundry in Coventry. I had to work the night shift and then come back to a cramped room with three other Punjabi men. We had a sink and a one bar electric heater. I had never felt cold like it and the snow, when it fell in the street, was nothing like the snow in the story book my cousin sent me.'

Tracy offered him her arm and took him to one of the cane chairs by the window. She drew up another seat next to him. 'How was it different?'

'It was dirty from the wheels of the vehicles and from people's feet. It never seemed to settle for long and the slush that sprayed up from the lorries and the vans, made it unpleasant to walk. Maybe it would have been different if I'd had a garden but by the time I had left the foundry, started up my own business and bought a house with more than just a tiny backyard, I had left that dream behind.'

Tracy stood up and put her hands in her apron pockets. 'That's a shame.'

'That is reality,' Mr Bhadu replied.

The day of the outing arrived and, with it, a strange stillness to the air. The sky, that had been blue when Tracy had left her parents' house that morning, was now grey and the cold was biting. Letting herself into the club house at The Cedars, she took off her coat and hung it over the coat stand. Rubbing her hands together, she went to find Mrs Derbyshire in the office.

She was checking the forecast on the computer. 'I'm not liking the look of this,' she said, glancing out of the window. 'It says it will be snowing heavily by lunch time. Just our luck on the day we go to the pantomime.'

'The forecasters get it wrong all the time. It might not even happen.'

'If it does, then we'll have to cancel the coach. We have to think of the health and safety of the residents. The roads will be treacherous and we don't want to be stranded at the theatre, do we?'

'I suppose not.'

Tracy went over to the roster on the wall, noticing, as she did, that the first flakes of snow had started to fall. By the time she'd found her name, it was starting to settle.

It continued to snow all day and by two o'clock the communal garden of The Cedars was white. An inch of snow lay on top of the bird feeders. The residents had gathered in the club lounge to find out what was happening and Tracy noticed how all eyes were on the snowy garden.

'That's it then. Pantomime's off.' There was more than a small amount of satisfaction in Gloria's voice as she rested her head against the sliding doors. 'Can't say I'm sorry.'

'It is beautiful though, isn't it?' Tracy said.

Gloria stared wistfully at the whirling flakes. 'It reminds me of when I was a girl. My dad used to…'

She was interrupted by Mrs Derbyshire who had come into the lounge with her clipboard.

'I'm sorry everyone. I know you're disappointed about the pantomime but I have lots of other ideas for things we can do this afternoon. As we're all together, I thought maybe a quiz or perhaps a singsong. Mr Bhadu, you know lots of...'

She stopped and looked around her. 'Has anyone seen Mr Bhadu?'

There was a collective shake of heads but just as Tracy was about to go and find him, the door opened and Mr Bhadu came into the lounge. He was holding a piece of paper in his hand.

'I have come to give you this, my dear,' he said, making his way over to Tracy and handing her the paper. 'It is my suggestion for our outing. I never put it in the box.'

Tracy unfolded the paper and read it. When she had finished, her face broke into a smile.

'I couldn't have thought of a better place myself. Come on everyone, get your coats on, we're going into the garden!'

Anyone passing The Cedars Retirement Village that afternoon would have wondered at the sight. Parveen and Mr Bhadu were putting the finishing touches to their snowmen and Jack and Gloria were engaged in a rather energetic snowball fight.

'Who said girls couldn't throw?' Gloria shouted as another hit Jack on the shoulder.

'Careful everyone... health and safety.' Mrs Derbyshire shouted from the terrace. But it was said so half-heatedly that no one took much notice.

'It was a good suggestion, Mr Bhadu,' Tracy said, watching him wind a spare turban around the snowman's head. 'At last we found something everyone wanted to do.'

Mr Bhadu stopped and looked at her, then he bent his head and lifted the string of the embroidered purse over his head.

'I would like you to have it, Tracy.'

'But I can't. It's your purse, Mr Bhadu. The one your wife gave you for your memories.'

With shaking hands, he placed the purse around her neck. 'Remember what Neeta said. That only when my memories of India and England were of equal weight would I shall be truly happy?'

'Yes.'

'Well, today,' he said, looking at his neighbours enjoying the snow, 'I put my last special memory of England in the purse. It has taken many years but it is full now and I am happy. You are young, with all your life ahead of you. Now it's your turn to fill the purse with memories. Maybe one day, you will travel or even find another place to live.'

Planting his stick in the snow to steady himself, he turned and started walking back to the house. 'Just like the birds in the garden.'

'Or like *you*, Mr Bhadu.'

Tracy didn't think he had heard her but as, he reached the terrace, the old man stopped.

'Yes,' he said, with a smile. 'Just like me.'

ALL I WANT FOR CHRISTMAS

The strange creature on the computer screen, with the orange fur and staring blue eyes, put his paws over his big furry belly.

'What's he doing?' Keith asked.

'He's telling me he's hungry,' Rachel replied.

'Oh dear. What are you going to do?'

'I'm going to take him to the on-line store and buy him some food of course. I've got lots of Rox to spend because I've been playing games and solving puzzles so I can look after him.'

'Oh, of course. Silly me,' Keith said, trying to keep the bafflement from his face.

'If I don't feed him and play with him, he'll be sad.'

'Yes, I suppose he will.'

Rachel was Jilly's seven year old daughter and when he had first met Jilly, Rachel had been only four. After their divorce, Rachel's father had moved to America and his visits were few and far between.

Keith had been keen to take up the shortfall: he had asked Jilly to marry him the previous spring and since their wedding in the summer, was doing his best to be a good father to the little girl.

'What exactly is it?' The creature was scratching and yawning.

'It's my Furi. He's a Moshi Monster. Look – I've made him a special home,' Rachel said, climbing onto his lap. 'Do you want to see him do some tricks?'

If Keith was perfectly honest, before that day he had never heard of a Moshi Monster.

'But how can you not have?' Jilly said later as they got ready for bed. 'It's all she and her friends have been playing for the last few months. I know it means she's in front of the computer but she's learning how to be responsible and make decisions – and recognising the consequences of those decisions.

Keith was not so sure. Shouldn't little girls be playing with dolls or dressing up in Disney Princess costumes or something? He disliked the idea of so much time being spent on the computer but at the end of the day, Jilly was Rachel's daughter and he didn't want to interfere. He was just pleased that Rachel seemed to have taken to him so easily, despite his lack of experience with young children.

The following day saw Keith braving the Christmas Eve crush.

'This should be easy,' he thought.

He pulled the collar of his coat up around his ears and wished that he had brought his woollen hat with him. The town was busy with late night shoppers and now and again he was forced to step into the road to avoid being bumped.

Half blinded by the sleet that had fallen relentlessly since he had left the office that evening, Keith pushed open the heavy door of the department store.

'This shouldn't take long.' He took a folded piece of paper out of his back pocket. Now what was the name of it again? He glanced at the paper. Ah yes, Moshi Monster – that was it.

He took the escalator to the toy department and stared at the signs that hung above each aisle: Board Games, Computer Games, Educational Toys. What aisle would it be in? There should be an aisle labelled, 'Toys for parents who have left their shopping until Christmas Eve'.

'This is silly,' he muttered. He had read that it was one of the top ten children's Christmas presents that year. Why couldn't he see it?

At last he found the shelf with the soft toys. There was Pepper Pig and The Gruffalo. There was Elmer and numerous assorted Pillow Pets and there, between the Toy Story Woodies and the Hello Kitties, was… the space where the Moshi Monsters should have been.

'I'm looking for a Moshi Monster soft toy. The one that's called Furi,' Keith said to an assistant who was re-stocking one of the shelves. 'Could you tell me where I could find one?'

The assistant shook her head. 'I'm afraid we've got none left. We sold out a couple of weeks ago. We were promised some new stock but it hasn't arrived yet. You might be lucky if you call back in a week or so.'

Keith rubbed the back of his neck. 'But that's no good. I need it for tomorrow – for Christmas.'

'Well, I'm sorry but I can't help you. Maybe you could try Marstons on the corner. They might still have some.

'Okay, thanks.'

Returning to the ground floor, Keith wound his scarf tightly round his neck and stepped back out into the street. The wind had picked up – whipping the ends of his coat and stinging his cheeks. He ducked his head against the sleet and ran across the road.

Marstons was a traditional toy shop. It had changed little since Keith was a boy spending his pocket money on Star War action figures.

'Hello there. I hope you're going to be able to help me. I need to find a Moshi Monster. If I'd realised that they were going to be sold out so quickly I'd never have left it so late.'

'I think you might be in luck,' the man behind the counter said, closing the order book he'd been writing in. 'We had a new delivery at the beginning of the week. They've been incredibly popular, you know – especially since the computer game took off.'

'So it seems. Anyway, where can I find them?'

Simon indicated the aisle behind him. 'Middle shelf down the end there.'

'Thanks.' Keith made his way down the aisle and looked along the shelves. He recognised the distinctive packaging straight away and was pleased to see at least four different monsters in their boxes.

'Now which one was it?' He moved from box to box. The first monster he saw was what he could only describe as a red and black creature in the shape of a volcano. No, that wasn't the one. The next contained a strange creature with spiky purple hair. That certainly wasn't it either and neither were the next two.

With racing heart, he took out his mobile phone. Jilly answered at the first ring. 'Hi, Jill. Look I can't find the Furi. I'm in Marstons and they seem to have every monster except that one. What shall I do? Shall I get her one of the others? No? Okay I'll keep looking. What's Rachel doing? Petting her Moshi Monster – what a surprise!'

Keith looked at his watch. Six thirty. The shops would be open later tonight to catch the last minute Christmas trade but he needed to be home by seven thirty at the latest. This would be their first Christmas together and he wasn't going to miss watching Rachel place her stocking on her bed. Last weekend he had helped her to write a letter to Santa. He had placed the note above the dancing flames in the fireplace and together they had watched it catch alight and disappear up the chimney.

He remembered the note, written in her childish hand. Furi Moshi Monster was top of the list.

'It talks and has an adoption certificate, you know,' she had told him. He would just have to keep looking. He didn't want to disappoint her – not on their first Christmas.

'The market,' Keith thought. 'That's the place.'

The wind had dropped and the sleet was turning to snow. Christmas lights twinkled in the bare branches of the trees around the market square and through the speakers, carols were playing. It was not as hectic here as on the high street; Keith had a good feeling about the place.

The striped canopies of the stalls were starting to sag with the weight of the settling snow as Keith made his way up and down the rows. He could see leather handbags, cushion covers, tinsel in all colours and thicknesses and rows of second hand books but no Moshi Monsters.

'That's it then,' he thought.

At the edge of the square was an iron bench. Keith walked over to it and brushed the snow off before sitting down heavily. Despite his thick coat, the metal was cold beneath his legs – so different from the spring evening when he had sat in this very same spot and asked Jilly to marry him.

That day the air had carried the heady scent of lilacs from nearby gardens and when she had said yes, he had felt invincible.

'I'll look after you both. I won't ever let you down,'

Jilly had laughed and said that she didn't need looking after but he had meant every word.

Only, of course this time he *had* let them down. He would have to go home empty handed and explain to his wife how he had failed to find the one thing that Rachel really wanted and listen to Jilly say that I didn't matter. He put his head in his hands... to him, it mattered a lot.

'Are you all right?' An elderly lady was standing in front of him with a perplexed expression. It was his neighbour Mrs Jennings. On the end of its lead, her little white terrier was snuffling under the bench in the hope of finding dropped food. 'You look rather upset. What seems to be the problem?'

She looked kindly down at Keith, who stood up awkwardly. 'Please, don't worry. I'm fine. Really I am.'

'Why don't you sit back down and tell me about it and we'll see if there isn't something to be done.'

Feeling foolish, he explained what had happened. 'It's really important that I get one before tomorrow. I don't want to let my daughter down.'

Keith swallowed and his eyes prickled. It was the first time he had called Rachel his daughter and he realised that it had just slipped out naturally.

'I know it's only a computer monster but she feeds it and looks after it and just loves caring for it. I wanted to get her the soft toy version so she could hug it as well. Isn't that what little girls love to do?'

'Well, this one did,' said Mrs Jennings, scooping up her dog and holding it close, 'and still does.'

'That's it!' Keith shouted and jumped off the bench.

Christmas morning arrived with the sound of Rachel dragging her stocking across the landing and into their bedroom. It was six o'clock.

She plonked herself on the end of the bed and pulled the stocking up after her. As she tore the paper from the presents, which Keith and Jilly had carefully wrapped the previous night, she squealed with delight.

'There's another present for you Rach,' Keith said. 'You'll need to go into the kitchen to find it, though.'

Rachel ran down the stairs, two at a time. In the kitchen was a large hutch with red tinsel around it. Inside was a lop-eared rabbit.

'It's not a Moshi Monster I'm afraid but Mum and I thought that as you have looked after your Furi so well, you've proved that you're old enough to care for a real pet.'

When Mrs Jennings had hugged her little dog, the idea had come to him. He had rushed over to the pet superstore and carefully chosen the cutest, fluffiest rabbit they had.

'The hutch can stay in the kitchen until the weather improves. I've got some leaflets on how to look after him, which we can read together.'

Rachel picked up the rabbit and held it to her chest. 'I'm going to call him Furi. He's the best present in the world.'

Jilly smiled at Keith and put her arm around him. 'This is as good a time as any to tell you.'

'What's that then?'

'We're going to be having a little Moshi Monster of our own,' she said.

'You mean…' Keith gave a whoop.

'Hush…I haven't told Rachel yet!'

Keith thought for a minute and then got up and went over to the computer.

'What are you doing, Keith?' Jilly asked.

'I'm going to feed the Moshi,' he said, with a smile. 'I'll need to get some practice in.'

CANCELLING CHRISTMAS

'What's the theme going to be this year?'

Yvonne craned her neck over the fence and grinned but Geraldine carried on down the path towards her car. Maybe if she pretended not to have heard, she could avoid this conversation.

'I reckon 2002 was the best,' her neighbour continued. 'When we all had to come as a Disney character. You were Cruella De Ville and you'd dressed the kids up as Dalmatians. Priceless.'

Geraldine had no option but to stop. 'That was 2003. 2002 was *Come as a Christmas Carol.*'

Yvonne counted on her fingers. 'You're right, you know. How many shepherds did you get that evening? Seven? eight?'

'Twenty-two,' Geraldine said, remembering the fairy lights on the lawn and the fake snow from the machine that had wowed their guests. 'Including the one with bare feet who said he was washing his socks by night.'

Yvonne laughed. 'You and Dan sure know how to throw a good party. I was only saying last night, to the girls at the book club, that in Elm Drive, we all count down the days until you tell us your party theme. They were really jealous – said that nothing festive goes on in their roads. So, go on give me a clue... just a little teensy one.'

'You'll be the first to know,' Geraldine said, ducking into her car and slamming the door. Damn. Why couldn't she have just told her that there would be no party this year. Or the next. That Christmases in the Davis household from now on would be different.

She and Dan had made the decision two weeks ago as they stared at the inflatable snowman and the sign that said *Park Here Santa*, which Dan had just carried down from the loft.

'What's the point?' she'd said, fingering the string of lights that framed the sign. 'Who are we doing it for, Dan? Now that we're going to be on our own at Christmas.'

For the last two decades and more, since their youngest, Helena, had been born, they had celebrated Christmas in style. The run up to the festivities had included family carol singing on the common; a secret Santa between the neighbours, organised by her eldest daughter Julia; a life-sized Santa and his sleigh, picked out in flashing Christmas lights on the roof and of course the snowman, with a little charity collection box next to him. People had been known to bring their children from several towns away to see the dazzling display.

But of course, Geraldine thought, easing her car out of the drive, each year all of this would be eclipsed by *the party*. It had become legendary in Elm Drive. How were they going to tell everyone that this year they'd be in sunny Spain?

Geraldine flipped through the brochure: kidney shaped pool, flamenco nights, tapas bars and sandy beaches. Dan stood behind her and rested his chin on her head.

'It's going to be great and the last-minute booking was a bargain. We should have done this years ago.'

'We couldn't have done, Dan. We had the kids, and Christmas is for children, after all. They would have hated being away from home.'

'I know they would... but that's all changed now, what with the girls being away. Did you see Helena's postcard? It came while you were out.' He indicated the bright picture of an elephant on the coffee table.

'Yes, I saw it. Sounds like she's having a great gap year. I'm just so pleased that Jed decided to go with her. I didn't like the idea of her travelling on her own.'

'Well, you know what they say,' Dan placed the holiday brochure back in the magazine rack and sat himself at the computer. 'A holiday can make or break a relationship.'

'Must you always think the worst, Dan.'

'Just being realistic. That's all.'

'By the way,' Geraldine said, glancing at the photos of her girls on the piano. 'Julia hasn't rung this week. Do you think she's all right?'

'Why shouldn't she be? It's a great company she works for. Wish I'd had such opportunities at her age. Think of all the tea parties she'll be having.'

'Very funny.' Geraldine couldn't help being concerned for her eldest daughter so far away in Boston, but Dan was right – the job was a dream come true for her. 'By the way, I met Martin in the supermarket. He asked when he could come over to string up the icicle lights across the front of our two houses. Yvonne forgot to mention it when I saw her earlier. I'd forgotten all about that – I didn't really know what to tell him.'

'So what *did* you say?'

'I told him that you'd have a word with him about it.'

'Great.' Dan ran a hand through his hair. 'I suppose I'd better go and see him later – make up some excuse. Have you cancelled the turkey at Rodney's yet?'

Geraldine shook her head. 'I thought I'd do it tomorrow on my way to work... and the veggie box. What do you think we should do about a tree this year?'

'I don't think we should do anything. What's the point of having it sit in the corner for two weeks dropping its needles. By the time we come back it will be nothing more than a skeleton.'

She knew her husband was right – it was the only practical thing to do – but there had never been a time that she could remember when they had been without a tree. Every year, in October, the family would drive to Caulder Wood and reserve a tree from the plantation. The children would take tinsel and home-made baubles and decorate it so they would recognise it again. Then they would count down the days until they could go back in December, cut it down and stand it in the window, where they would dress it in its finery – as proud as parents at a christening.

'Traditions,' Geraldine sighed.

'What was that?' Dan raised his head from the computer where he was filling out their holiday insurance form.

'Oh, nothing,' she said.

'I can't do it. I can't tell them.'

A week had gone by and still Geraldine had said nothing to their neighbours. It was only three days before their flight. She put Dan's tea cup on the bedside table and climbed back into bed.

'Then don't.'

'Don't what?'

Dan took a sip of his tea. 'Don't tell them. We'll just go away on Wednesday and that way by the time we come back, it will all be over and everyone will have forgotten about Christmas.'

'But they're all going to be so disappointed. Mrs Guthrie at number 21 said that she'd found some white fur material in the charity shop and was sure that, whatever our party theme, she'd be able to make something out of it.'

'Then she can make it for something else. We can't live our Christmas around other people, Geraldine. We've done our bit... more than our bit... we deserve a rest from it and Spain is a good place to start.'

'But what about the party? Everyone expects it.'

'I think that says it all. This year Christmas is officially cancelled.' Dan opened the Sunday paper and Geraldine took that as a signal that the conversation had come to an end.

Geraldine's breath hung white in the cold air. It was seven in the evening and Dan had just put the last case in the boot.

'That's it then.' She looked at the house. Its dark windows looked back at her bare and blank. Up and down Elm Drive, Christmas lights twinkled from the eaves of the houses and fir trees peeped from behind part closed curtains.

Geraldine shivered. 'I miss all this.'

'There's nothing to miss.' Dan opened the passenger door for her. 'Just silly traditions and false festivities.'

'I didn't know you thought that?'

Her husband pulled up his collar and climbed into the driver's seat. 'Well, you do now,' he said, before putting the car into first and pulling away with an uncharacteristic squeal of tires.

The airport was busy with people making last minute getaways to the sun.

'Do you know which is our check in desk?'

'I think it's this one.' They both stared glumly at the line of people snaking up and down the roped aisles.

'Maybe we should have got here earlier.' Dan massaged his brow with the heel of his hand. He didn't like queues. 'I wish we'd had something to eat before we came out.'

'Look, why don't you stay in the queue with the cases and I'll go and find us a coffee and a sandwich – we can eat while we're waiting.'

'Sounds like a plan,' Dan said. He wheeled the cases to the end of the line and sat down on one of them.

Geraldine turned to walk away then hesitated a moment. 'Don't you think it's odd that we haven't heard anything from Julia. She said she'd ring and let us know her plans. Last I heard, she was going to be staying with a friend in Vermont but, chances are, that will all have changed.'

'Well, you know Julia. As fickle as the British weather.'

Geraldine laughed and went in search of a cafe.

When her phone rang, Geraldine had a Styrofoam cup of coffee in each hand and a bag of rolls under one arm. She put the coffees on the floor and dug into her bag for her mobile.

'Helena!' Her daughter's voice was barely audible through the crackly line. 'What was that? The line's really bad, Helena. You say you've run out of money?'

The idea had been for her daughter to supplement her travel money with bar jobs but this obviously hadn't gone to plan. 'Do you want me to wire you some?'

She listened without comment, as her daughter told her how homesick she'd been and how she had fallen out with Jed. When the call had ended, she sank to the floor beside the coffees. Jed was staying in Thailand but Helena was coming home early... for Christmas.

By the time she reached their check in desk, the queue had shortened dramatically but Dan didn't appear to be in it. Maybe he'd already checked in the bags.

'Over here, Geraldine.'

She wheeled around. Dan was sitting by a pillar, their cases beside him. His mobile was in his hand.

'What are you doing? Why have you left the queue?'

'I tried to ring you but your phone was engaged.'

Geraldine's heart sank. 'I know, Dan. It was Helena. She...'

Dan put up a hand to stop her. 'I had a call from Julia.'

Geraldine's hand sprung to her mouth and for a moment she forgot her news. 'How is she? What did she say?'

Dan fixed her with his brown eyes. 'That she's catching the evening flight and will be at Heathrow late tomorrow morning.'

'Heathrow!'

'That's what she said. Apparently, she's met some guy at the office named Scott and, Julia being Julia, is convinced he's *the one*. She's told him all about our traditions – the tree and the carol singing and, of course, the famous parties and he wants to come over and experience them himself. He's an only child, apparently, and didn't have a particularly happy childhood so Julia wants to show him what hers was like.'

Geraldine looked at Dan's weary expression. They both knew that their Christmas plans were about to take another turn. 'I've some news too,' she said. 'It's Helena.'

Geraldine and Dan sat at the kitchen table eating breakfast. The cases stood in the hall where they'd left them the previous evening.

'I'm sorry, Dan. I know how much you wanted this holiday.'

Dan shrugged. 'Well, you know what they say — the best laid plans and all that.'

'Julia's arriving first. Her flight's due in at eleven tomorrow morning. By the time they've been through customs, collected their luggage and picked up the hire car, I reckon it will be about one.' Geraldine calculated in her head. 'With a two hour drive, they should be here by three. That gives us eight hours.'

Dan swallowed his cornflakes. 'For what?'

Geraldine patted him on the shoulder. 'To organise Christmas!'

'This is the best party yet. How clever of you to think up a *'Come in whatever you were wearing when you received the invitation'* party.'

Yvonne emptied her glass and placed it on the table. She smoothed the baby doll nightdress over her knees. Geraldine laughed. Considering she'd put the invitation through her neighbour's door at ten o'clock that morning, she thought it unlikely that this was what Yvonne had been wearing.

She looked around the room. Don from number six was wearing his golfing sweater and had leant a club against the wall. Clare and Rob from Bramble Cottage had on matching chefs aprons and their son, Gary, had a towel wrapped around his waist. Mrs Guthrie had turned her white fur from the charity shop into a little bolero.

'I wasn't exactly wearing it when I got the invitation but I was sewing it so I reckon that's just as good... and I did so want to wear it,' she had said.

Now, she saw Helena heading towards her. Her rucksack bounced on her back and her legs looked tanned in her shorts.

'Think it's all right if I take it off now?' She shrugged the rucksack off her shoulder and gave Geraldine a hug.

She hugged her back and then held her daughter at arms length.

'Are you sure you're all right, darling.'

Helena nodded. 'I'm fine Mum. If Jed and I hadn't travelled together, we'd still be thinking we were right for each other. It's so good to be home though – Christmas wouldn't be Christmas without all this. It's a great party Mum.'

'It sure is, Mrs Davis.' Geraldine jumped. She hadn't noticed the tall, tanned young man who had come up beside her. Her daughter Julia hung from his arm. Geraldine watched Scott as he looked around the room, his eyes stopping at the six foot tree in the window that Dan had managed to buy at the supermarket. It was covered in all the decorations she and the girls had made over the years. Several people had grouped themselves around the piano and were singing carols. She and Dan had asked everyone to bring one piece of Christmas food and the dining table was groaning.

He nodded appreciatively. 'You sure do know how to have fun at Christmas time.'

'Yes, we do, don't we.' Geraldine smiled, then turned to Yvonne who was eyeing the young man with interest. 'I'd like you to meet Yvonne, Scott. She's a neighbour of ours.'

Yvonne offered her hand to the young man then turned to Julia. 'Your mum's such a clever thing, holding a surprise party. We didn't know what was going on. Tricked us well and good.' She laughed and pointed a finger at Dan, who had come to join them, a tray of mulled wine in his hands. 'Been all secretive... both of them... thought they'd run away or something!'

Dan caught Geraldine's eye and winked. The room was filled with the happy sound of laughter and chat. She looked around at her friends and family and realised what they would have missed if they had gone to Spain and she knew that Dan felt it too.

She took her husband's hand, glad that he'd remembered to hide the suitcases in the garage, then smiled at Yvonne.

'Cancel Christmas?' She wagged a finger at her neighbour. 'Shame on you, Yvonne... How could you have thought such a thing.'

THE GREATEST GIFT

David stood outside the department store and pressed his hands against the frosted glass. The window display was as spectacular as usual – a Dickensian scene complete with a mannequin Scrooge, Tiny Tim and a table laden with food.

The rest of the window contained an artful display of merchandise from the store: a wok, alongside a book showing a hundred and one ways to cook with noodles; pink hair straighteners; a set of stainless steel pans and a hamper full of jars of chutneys and packs of smoked salmon. There was even a set of dumbbells. In fact, there was every present you could ever wish to give that special person in your life… unless you were David.

The problem was, he'd already had his Christmas present. He'd been blessed with the most beautiful and amazing gift of all – his girlfriend Lindsay. He'd met her six months ago and, although he thought he was punching above his weight, he had plucked up the courage to ask her out. When she had agreed, and they'd had a pretty nice time, he had asked her out again.

As the summer had turned to autumn and then winter, they had started to see each other regularly and to his amazement, despite his incurable untidiness, two children who visited every second weekend and an inability to say what he felt, she seemed to like him too! What's more, despite his nervousness at their first meeting, Lindsay and his boys had hit it off. Yes, life was good. Or rather it would be, if it wasn't for the question of the present. This would be their first Christmas together and it was important that he buy Lindsay something that showed her how much she meant to him.

Through the brightly-lit window, David watched the animated Scrooge shake his head in sympathy as his flesh-coloured fiberglass hand carved the turkey.

'Think you have problems, mate?'

What should he buy? That was the question he had been asking himself for the last few weeks and scouring the internet and numerous trips to the shops hadn't helped to answer it. In the end he'd given up and, while they were out walking one day, had simply asked Lindsay what she wanted.

She'd just given him one of her amused smiles. 'Don't worry about getting me anything. Save your money for the children.'

That's what he loved most about her, the way she thought of everyone before herself.

'I've already given Sonia some money to put towards the new PlayStation they want but I can't just give *you* money.'

He was deadly serious but she'd just laughed. 'It's the thought behind the gift that counts. Look, David, if you're that worried you can always buy something and save the receipt – that way we can take it back if I don't like it.'

He wanted her to like it though. That was the problem.

As David turned away from the shop window, he almost bumped into a small boy who was standing in the middle of the pavement. He was wearing a padded blue jacket and as he lifted his arms up to his mother, David could see the tears running down his face.

'I've lost Blue Bear,' he sobbed.

Picking him up, the young woman looked back the way they'd come, her eyes searching the pavement for the lost toy. When she couldn't see it, she tenderly wiped away her son's tears with her thumb and kissed his cheek. 'Don't worry,' she said. 'We'll go back and find him.'

With an apology to David for having held him up, they disappeared into the throng of last minute shoppers, leaving David to his thoughts. Maybe he could buy Lindsay a scarf... or some jewellery. From what he could remember though, the only jewellery he had ever seen her wear was a thin gold chain around her neck and he suspected a scarf would be something that would end up pushed to the back of a drawer.

He'd never been much good at buying presents. When he was a child his mother had bought them all for him and as he got older, he had bribed his sister to take on the task – it was amazing what an offer of a meal at Nandos could achieve.

This, though, was different. The true meaning of Christmas, he knew, was in the giving and it was up to him to find the perfect present. A memory came to him. He was around seven or eight and he could still feel the excitement of rushing down the stairs on Christmas morning and wondering whether the largest present under the tree might be his. Yes, Lindsay's present must be as big as his love for her. A car, maybe… or a washing machine.

Realising that he was getting carried away, and that the high street was offering up little in the way of inspiration, David wandered in the direction of the covered shopping centre. It was Christmas Eve and if he didn't find something soon he would have nothing to give her.

The town was busy and he had to step off the pavement to make way for an elderly man who was pushing his wife in a wheelchair. As they passed by, the blanket that was covering the woman's knees slipped to the ground and the man stopped to pick it up. He gently tucked it around her once more and they carried on their way but not before David had seen the tender look his wife had given him in return. It gave him a warm feeling inside.

The more David walked the more he saw: a young husband with a protective arm around the shoulders of his pregnant wife; a grandfather teasing his young grandson; a teenage boy, with arms covered in tattoos, cradling a baby. At the end of the road, he stopped. It had come to him in a flash – the perfect gift.

The Christmas dinner had been eaten and the washing up done. Sonia would be over to collect the boys later and they had all gathered around the tree to open their gifts.

'This one's for you,' David said, handing Lindsay a carefully wrapped present.

Lindsay opened it. Lifting the book from its wrapping. '*One hundred and one ways to cook with noodles*! That's handy.'

'It's not what I wanted to get. I just couldn't...'

But she'd stopped him with a kiss. 'No, really – I mean it. It's a great present. How about I make something delicious out of it for the kids next time we're all here? A special meal for my favourite people.'

Such warmth and openness. As David watched Lindsay and his boys flip through the pages, deciding on what looked a good choice, he knew that the present he had saved for later was the perfect choice.

'It's been a wonderful day.' Lindsay leant her head against David's shoulder. 'Thank you for inviting me to share it with you.'

David had lit the fire and they sat side by side on the settee, watching the lights from the Christmas tree twinkle in the darkened room. The children had gone and in other years David would have felt an emptiness – but not this year.

'It's me who should be thanking *you*. I have a present for you, Lindsay.'

Lindsay turned her head and looked at him. 'But you've already given me a present.'

David stroked her hair. 'That was just an extra. This present is the proper one... but before I give it to you, I must tell you one thing about it.'

'What's that?'

'This gift doesn't have a receipt and it can't be taken back. It's a present to show how much you mean to me.'

Lindsay smiled. 'Now I'm intrigued.'

David held out his hands, palms upwards to her. 'This is for you.'

'What is it?' Lindsay looked confused.

'It's my love, Lindsay. You were right. A gift doesn't have to cost a lot or be in the biggest box and tied with a fancy bow. What I'm trying to say is, I love you… and if you'll have me, I'd like to marry you.'

In the end, it had been easy to find Lindsay the perfect present. He had seen it in the touch of a mother's thumb wiping away her child's tears, the smile of an elderly woman for her husband and the protective arms of a new father.

He bent his head and kissed her. 'I'm just sorry it's taken me so long to say it.'

CHRISTMAS STRIKE

'That's it. Enough is enough.'

Jan stared at the sink full of washing up that hadn't been put in the dishwasher and the plates and cups, on the kitchen table that, hadn't made it even that far.

It wasn't that she felt any more or less tired after her day at work, just that in less than twenty-four hours, Brian's mother was coming to stay for Christmas. And Brian's mother staying meant the whole house would need to be cleaned. Vera had been widowed for nearly thirty years and was the only person she knew who would run her finger across the slats in the blind when she thought nobody was looking.

'Who dusts blinds?' she had asked her husband once.

'My mother,' he'd replied, as if it explained everything.

She and Brian had hoped that with the coming of grandchildren, Vera would soften. Instead it seemed to make her worse and, in time, the kids had stopped trying to show her their pictures or ask her to play with their games. Afraid they'd be turned away.

'You were never allowed to bring your toys downstairs, Brian,' she would say. 'The living room was for adult conversation.'

Jan would bristle with irritation but Brian would only shrug and start picking up Libby's toys from the living room floor.

Christmas was the worst time and soon they came to dread her arrival. She would complain about the needles which dropped from the tree and on Christmas morning, as the children ripped the paper off their gifts, she would tut and mutter about wastage. So when, one year, Vera announced she was going be spending Christmas at her sister's instead, they had all breathed a guilty sigh of relief.

'What were Christmases like being an only child, Brian?' Jan had asked, trying to picture him as a boy in the neat semi-detached house, complete with artificial Christmas tree, where Vera now lived alone.

'Lonely,' he had replied.

It was hard to imagine that the next day her mother-in law would be arriving. Her sister was in hospital, having had a fall, and, in a moment of Christmas spirit, they had invited Vera to stay with them instead. As she walked into the living room, and looked around her, Jan wondered if it was a decision she would live to regret.

Jan was used to being the one who tried to keep their home in some sort of order but, as she took in the chaos, something hardened. The room looked like a refugee camp. Charlotte's pink duvet trailed from the arm of the settee and the remains of a fish and chip supper lay in its oil-soaked newspaper – presumably Harry hadn't been able to wait until she came home to cook him something.

In the middle of all this, her youngest daughter, Libby, sat like a bride, in a sea of snowflake confetti. With a look of concentration on her face, she attempted to cut another shape out of the paper with her blunt-ended scissors.

'Hi, Mummy. What's for tea?'

From Charlotte's room upstairs, Beyoncé was singing about single ladies and as she thought of her chaotic family, she found herself nostalgic for those long ago carefree days before marriage and children.

Why wasn't Charlotte helping Libby? So much for asking her to look after her sister until she got back from work. And as for her husband – what had possessed him to book a business trip on the eve of his mother's arrival? The whole house needed to be cleaned from top to bottom and she felt overwhelmed by the enormity of the task ahead of her.

'Clear up now, Libby.'

Her daughter looked up from her sea of paper, her face showing her surprise, and Jan realised her words had come out sharper than she'd intended.

'Can you help me, Mum?'

'Can't you do it yourself?'

Libby picked up some snowflakes and dropped them. 'I suppose so.'

There was some cold chicken in the fridge. Jan put it onto two plates and added some salad and leftover cold potatoes. It would have to do for the girls' supper. She felt too tired to cook. Picking up one of the plates, she went upstairs and knocked on Charlotte's door.

'Did you remember Granny Vera's coming tomorrow evening and you're to share with Libby?'

Make up covered the bedspread and the floor was littered with the grinning faces of the models that graced the covers of Charlotte's favourite magazines. Jan tried to picture her mother-in-law sleeping there and failed.

'Of course I did, Mum. I'm not senile.'

Jan sighed, feeling suddenly very tired. When she spoke again, her voice didn't sound her own.

'And the tree, Charlie… You said you and Harry would decorate it.'

'Chill, Mum. We can do it tomorrow.'

'No we can't! Granny Vera is arriving tomorrow afternoon!' She counted to ten to calm herself. 'Libby is having her supper and then I'd like you to put her to bed. I have a headache coming on and will see you in the morning.'

Jan walked out of the room and closed the door but not before she had seen her daughter glance at the fluorescent numbers of her digital clock and heard her surprised voice.

'But it's only eight o'clock, Mum.'

The next morning, Libby was first up. She dragged her blanket to her mother's bedroom door, as she usually did, then stopped. Something wasn't right. For one thing, the door was closed but there was also something stuck to it. Reaching up on tiptoe, she pulled the note down and stared at it. She'd only just learnt to read but the words, written in bold marker pen, were easy enough to work out.

On Strike!

Libby stood for a moment, with her thumb in her mouth and her hand raised to the door handle, uncertain as to whether she should go in. Instead, she went to look for her sister. When she found her, wrapped in her duvet, her mobile phone stuck to her ear, Libby was reminded of one of the pupae they'd been looking at in their science lesson.

'What do you want?' Charlotte glared at her sister. 'I'm talking to Scott.'

Libby dawdled in the doorway. 'Mum says she's on strike.'

'What do you mean? Look go away, Libby. I'm trying to have a private conversation.'

Libby ignored her and handed her the cardboard sign. 'There. Told you.'

She wasn't sure what the words meant but she liked the idea that she had been the first to find them.

'She's just having a laugh. You know how Mum likes to do everything for us. Now shut the door and go away... Sorry Scott what were you saying?'

Disappointed by her sister's reaction, Libby decided to try Harry. She pushed his bedroom door open enough to put her head around. She didn't like going into her brother's room as it smelt of old socks and stale sandwiches and she was never sure what she might tread on if she went in.

Harry was still in bed, a mound under his duvet. In the half light, Libby could just see the top of his curly head.

'Harry,' she whispered, stepping over a pile of clothes and a plate with what looked like the remains of a pizza on it. 'Harry, wake up.'

The mound stirred and her brother's bleary eyes peered over the covers. 'What is it, squirt?'

'Mum's on strike.'

Harry lifted his head a little in order to see her better. 'What do you mean, Mum's on strike? On strike from what?'

'I don't know,' Libby said, plonking herself on the end of Harry's bed, 'but I think it might be bad.'

Of course Libby had no way of knowing if this was true or not but she was happy to see that it made her brother sit up and rub his eyes. 'What does it mean, Harry?'

He looked at the note. 'I guess it means that Mum isn't going to do the things that Mum always does.'

'Like what?'

'I dunno – like pick up our clothes and put our plates in the dishwasher. Stuff like that.'

'But she's always done it.' Libby was pretty certain that her mother's strike was not going to be a good thing. 'I'm hungry.'

Harry scratched his head, making his hair stand on end. 'Get something to eat then.'

'I can't reach the cupboard. Mum usually gets the box down for me.'

'Can't you stand on a chair or something?'

'Mum says I'm not allowed.'

'It's that or go hungry,' her brother said, swinging his legs over the side of the bed and putting his foot in a bowl that had contained yesterday's coco pops. He wiped the chocolate coloured milk from his foot with the edge of his duvet and Libby giggled. Pulling his dressing gown over his boxers, Harry followed Libby onto the landing.

As they stood side by side outside their mum's room, Charlotte put her head around her door. She was still wrapped in her duvet and her face showed traces of the previous night's make up.

'She's still in there then? I wanted to borrow her make up remover wipes.'

'Maybe we should knock,' Libby said, putting her ear to the door. 'Grandma Vera's coming today for Christmas.'

'She was in a really funny mood yesterday,' Charlotte said. She glanced at the note in Harry's hand. 'You know… I think she might mean it.'

Libby waited for her to do something but it soon became clear that she didn't want to be the one to disturb their mother either. Instead, she took Libby by the hand and led her downstairs. She took the box of Shreddies from the cupboard and emptied it into three bowls.

'So what are we going to do?' Harry said, pulling out a chair. 'Granny will be here in a few hours and Dad won't be back until after lunch.'

Libby looked up at him, milk around her mouth. 'We could do it ourselves.'

'Do what ourselves?'

'You know – the stuff Mum always does before Granny arrives.'

Harry looked doubtful. 'I don't know where Mum keeps the Hoover.'

Charlotte pulled open a drawer that contained foil and bin liners. 'Or the dusters.' She shook her head and scanned the kitchen. 'What we need is someone who is good at tidying up and cleaning. Someone who enjoys it.'

'Someone like Granny Vera?' Libby said.

When Jan woke, the sun was streaming through the curtains. Looking at her clock, she saw it was past eleven – she must have been even more tired the previous evening than she thought. Surprised to hear the sound of the vacuum cleaner on the stairs, she got out of the bed and put her ear to the door. Every now and again there were snatches of voices and she thought she could hear the distant hum of the dishwasher in the kitchen.

Her mind was working overtime; she could just picture the scene. Harry would have overfilled the washing machine and the soapy water was probably, at this very minute, escaping from the tub and onto the floor; Charlotte would have knocked two plates together loading the dishwasher and Libby... well, it was probably better not to think about what her youngest might have done.

She knew it was all her own fault. When the children were young, instead of teaching them how to be responsible for their toys and respectful of their rooms, she'd be on the floor with them building forts out of Duplo or at the kitchen table making models out of home-made playdough. She had not equipped them for an independent life. How on earth would Harry survive when he started university next year?

The *On Strike* sign had just been a joke but she couldn't help wondering how they might be managing without her. She was about to leave her room, when she stopped with her hand on the door knob. Maybe she'd just leave them to it for half an hour or so and then, when she had viewed the chaos they had left in their cleaning wake, she would take over. Climbing back into bed, she closed her eyes. Later, she would phone Vera and postpone her visit until the afternoon.

When Jan woke again, the house was silent. She pushed her hair out of her eyes. How long had she been asleep? Swinging her legs over the side of the bed, she listened but could hear nothing. She walked over to the door and looked out. The landing was empty but the air smelt strange. What was it? Lavender?

As she made her way downstairs, she noticed that the fingerprints had been wiped off the wall. The stair carpet looked different too – no longer dark with cat hair. Glancing back at her door, she saw the *On Strike* sign had gone. Joke or not, the message seemed to have got through. She should have done this months ago... years even.

As she stood in the hall, she heard voices coming from the kitchen. The door was ajar and it was only when saw her mother-in law-sitting at the kitchen table that she realised she'd forgotten to ring her. She'd obviously decided to turn up early and there wasn't a thing she could do about it.

Through the half-open door, she could see Libby sitting cross-legged on the floor. The entire contents of one of the kitchen cupboards was laid out in front of her. As Jan watched, she held up a tin to her grandmother.

'Put the tinned peas with the sweetcorn, Libby. Yes, that's right, dear... and the baby carrots. The pears go with the mandarin oranges.'

'This is fun. Can we do the cereal cupboard next, Granny? I can never reach the Shreddies.'

'Most definitely.' Vera smiled and patted her head. 'And then we can stick your beautiful snowflakes on the window. But first I promised Charlotte that I'd help her sort her wardrobe.'

Taking a deep breath. Jan walked into the room. 'Vera... When did you get here?' She looked down at her dressing gown waiting for the inevitable criticism.

'Well, I got here as soon as Harry rang me.'

'Harry rang you?'

'Yes. He told me you weren't feeling well and had taken to your bed. He asked if I'd come round a bit earlier and help tidy up. I came straight away.'

As Vera spoke, she took the cans that Libby was holding out to her and started to arrange them neatly on the shelf. 'We've already done his room. Did you know your son has a collection of old Dandy comics? His grandfather used to collect them too. In fact, there might still be some in the attic – I'll look them out for him if you like.'

Jan fiddled with the tie of her dressing gown. 'I'm sure he'd like that.'

'We've filed them in date order,' Vera continued, then her face softened. 'He's grown up to be a fine young man, Janet.'

Jan had never heard Vera talk like this about any of her children. Was she still asleep? Was this a dream?

'Morning, Mum.' Charlotte brushed past her, holding a drawer full of makeup. She held it out to her grandmother.

Vera's eyes lit up. 'Put it over there, Charlie. We'll have that sorted in a jiffy. What you need are dividers – that way you can keep your eyes shadows separate from your lipsticks. I'll bring them next time I come.'

'Gran's been great, Mum. She found the homework I lost last week – it was under the bed.'

'Where's Harry?'

Vera glanced out of the window. 'Oh, I sent him to the Chinese on the corner for a takeaway – we were all much too busy to think about cooking.'

Jan watched Vera put the tins back in the cupboard. 'You didn't need to do this, Vera.'

Vera paused, her hand resting on the worktop. Her back was to her. 'I wanted to.'

'You did?'

'When Harry rung, I could hear the worry in his voice.' Her voice faltered. 'If I'm honest, Janet, it was nice to feel needed.'

Vera turned around and Jan noticed her eyes were tinged with red. For the first time, it occurred to her that Brian's mother might be lonely.

'You probably don't know this but Jack and I always wanted a large family.'

'No, I didn't know.' Jan tried to cover her surprise.

'Yes, after Brian we tried for another baby but after the second miscarriage we stopped. I put my efforts instead into becoming the perfect housewife. I realise now how hard it must have been for Brian. When he went to boarding school, he must have felt as though we were packing him away – just like his toys.'

'I'm sure he didn't think that.'

'Whenever I came to stay, your house would be full of laughter and mess. I complained about it but, deep inside, I knew that you concentrated on what was important – your children. It made me realise what I had missed out on. I was jealous and I'm afraid it made me rather harsh on you.'

When she looked at her, Jan saw in her eyes the sadness Vera had kept so well hidden.

'I'm so sorry. I never realised.'

'No, it's me who should be sorry, dear. Christmases were not the same without you all.'

'We're glad you came, Granny,' Libby climbed into Vera's lap and Jan realised it was the first time she'd done so.

'Yes, Gran. You're cool,' Charlotte said. 'I like my room much better now that I can find everything.'

Jan smiled at Vera, 'I think you've taught me a thing or two today too. It seems that the children like a little order in their lives after all.'

When Brian arrived home, the room was filled with the distinctive aroma of a Chinese take away. The table was covered in silver cartons and prawn crackers. He went over to his mother and gave her a dutiful kiss on the cheek.

'We saved you some,' Jan said. 'It's keeping warm in the oven.'

'I tried to get home as quickly as I could after Charlotte called – she told me about the stri...'

'Stripy dress,' Charlotte cut in, giving her dad a meaningful stare. 'The one that she wants to wear to your work's Christmas do.'

Brian looked confused. 'But I thought…'

'Don't worry,' Jan said. 'I'll explain later. Now I've an idea. How about we all decorate the Christmas tree… together.'

Vera smiled. 'I'd like that very much.'

Brian's eyebrows raised in surprise. 'You would?'

'Most definitely.'

Libby gave a loud whoop and Jan felt a warmth grow inside her as the little girl went over and took her grandmother's hand.

They all filed into the living room but Jan lingered. Something on the table had caught her eye. Pushed inside one of the empty takeaway bags, waiting to be taken out to the rubbish, was her *On Strike!* sign.

Glancing at the door, she shoved it further inside and smiled to herself. 'Hopefully, I won't be needing that again.'

FINDING SANTA

'This is a passenger announcement. Flight number EZY8667 is now boarding. Would passengers please make their way to gate number twenty-one.'

'Is it time to go?' Emma pulled at her mother's coat sleeve with her free hand. In the other, she tightly grasped the handle of her Mini Mouse case on wheels.

Marie looked down at her daughter's eager face. 'No, Emma. It's not our turn yet. That's someone else's plane.'

The waiting area of Gatwick South Terminal was so busy you would have been excused for thinking it was midsummer but outside the large picture windows, Marie could see the sky was darkening again and the flurries of snow they had met on their way up to the airport in the coach, were falling more heavily. She could only just make out the outline of the planes lined up on the tarmac.

It was Christmas Eve and she, along with hundreds of other families, were trying to escape the grey weather that had dogged England since early October. All around her, people were seated or stretched out on the metal benches; newcomers had to pick their way around an obstacle course of rucksacks and cabin bags.

'Do you think that Santa will know where we are?'

'Yes, of course he will. He knows where every child is.'

'But how will he know? What if he hasn't got the right address?'

Marie fought a desire to say, 'Because I told you so.'

Emma had been asking the same question since they had left the house that morning and, after their early start, the day already seemed very long. She wished that Lorna would take more notice of her sister – play a game of I spy or something.

She looked at her eldest daughter hunched in her chair, iPod plugged into her ears. A muted thud could just be heard and Marie had to restrain herself from yanking on the white cables and telling her that she would damage her ears. Why could she never seem to get away from the echoes of her own mother's voice?

Her phone beeped; probably another text from John. They were all the same: telling her he loved her and that he'd never meant to hurt her. She had deleted the last three and was determined not to read it.

She realised that Emma was still waiting for an answer. 'It's a kind of magic, Emma. He has a very special type of address book. Now how about looking at the new book we bought you?'

She rummaged in the carrier bag, full of sweets and magazines, for the books she'd bought for the journey. Marie hoped that 'Matilda' might win her some precious time away from the Santa questions. She was wrong.

'Why doesn't Santa bump into all the planes in the sky, Mum?'

'This is an announcement for passengers of Monarch flight: ZB 284. This flight has been delayed.'

'Oh, no! Please, not a delay.'

Marie glanced up at the flight information board as if it might somehow prove the announcement to be a mistake. No mistake.

Emma ran a plump hand over the fuzzy material of her seat. 'This is scratching my legs, Mum. When can we get on the plane?'

'It won't be long now. Try and be patient.'

'Ok. You be the doctor and I'll pretend I've got a bad leg. Then we can swap over.'

Marie sighed. 'Not that sort of patient, Emma. Come on. Let's look at the snow.'

She took her younger daughter's hand and led her to the viewing window. The snow had begun to settle and the runway was turning white. Through the ice crystals on the window, Marie could see a mantle of white covering the outstretched wings of the planes.

The holiday to Tenerife had seemed a good idea when she had booked it. A special Christmas just for the three of them. No mother telling her how she should be bringing up her daughters, no turkey to cook and no phone calls from John.

The hotel had promised sun, a kidney shaped pool and a children's club which Marie knew Emma would love. The hotel also had a disco – wasn't that just what sixteen year olds wanted from a holiday? Lorna hadn't seemed too enthusiastic when she had mentioned it, though.

'Will it be snowing on our holiday? Can we build a snowman?'

Marie let out a loud breath. 'No, Emma. It will be lovely and sunny. Remember I told you about the beach and the pool?'

Marie felt her stomach rumble and realised that it was long past lunch time. How long had they been at the airport? She calculated four hours. They walked back to their seat and Marie opened the packet of sandwiches she'd made that morning.

'Why is that man crying, Mum?' Emma said, as Marie handed her a sandwich.

Marie glanced over at a young lad on the seat opposite. His nose was red and a guitar case was balanced against the seat.

'He's not crying; he's just blowing his nose. He's probably got a cold.'

'Can I say hello to him, Mum.'

'I suppose so but don't make a nuisance of yourself.'

Emma hopped off her seat and plumped next to him. Where did she get such confidence? So unlike her sister who chose friends carefully and often preferred her own company. The boy looked startled.

'It's all right, she's with me,' Marie said.

Emma held out a sandwich. 'Do you want one? They're jam.'

'No thanks.' He looked at the sandwich suspiciously.

'Do you have a cold?'

'Yes. Don't sit too close; you don't want to catch it.'

'My mum said you did but I said you were crying.'

The boy stifled a smile.

'What's your name? I'm Emma.'

He slowly turned back towards her. 'Jake.'

'How old are you?'

'Nineteen.'

'Mum says I'm six going on thirteen, but I don't know what she means. My mum's thirty-six. That's my mum. She sometimes cries too when she thinks I'm not looking. '

He glanced at Marie who had caught her breath.

'I expect she had a cold too,' he said and Marie mouthed a silent thank you.

Emma pointed to the guitar case. 'What's that for?'

'I'm in a band. We were due to do a gig in one of the bars in Tenerife tonight.'

'What's a gig?'

'You know, like a small concert. It would have been my first one and I was really looking forward to it.'

'That's my sister over there. She likes singing too but only horrid loud stuff like... *Nothing else matters...bam bam bam.*' As she sang, she flipped her hair over her face and banged her head up and down.

Jake looked over at where Lorna was lying across three seats, pretending not to listen. When she realised she was being watched, she pulled the edges of her hooded jacket closer around her face and closed her eyes, but not before she had caught his slow smile. He leaned across and took one earpiece from Lorna's ear, putting it in his own before she could protest.

'What are you listening to? ... Metallica... cool.'

Hopping down from her chair, Emma opened her Mini Mouse case and took out some paper and a crayon. 'I'm going to write a Christmas wish list to Santa.'

'This is a passenger announcement for flight ZB284 to Tenerife. This flight has now been cancelled.'

Marie felt the disbelief in the air erupt into a wave of chaos and noise.

She walked over to the flustered holiday rep. A crowd had formed around her and everyone seemed to be talking at once.

'I'm really sorry but it's out of my control.' The woman held up her hands to a red-faced man who was demanding that she do something. Her face was flushed and she dabbed at the perspiration at the sides of her nose. 'The snow is four inches deep on the runway and we have been told that no flights will be taking off this evening. The airline has advised us that passengers should remain in the terminal building and await further instruction. Refreshment vouchers can be used in all the restaurants and bars.'

Marie couldn't help feeling sorry for the woman. After all, the snow was hardly her fault. She looked worriedly from Emma, happily writing, to Lorna and Jake, joined by the white cable of the iPod, tapping their feet in unison but they looked happy enough.

Lorna raised her eyes. Even though Metallica was pumping through her earphones, she was aware of the change in atmosphere. People were standing up and talking animatedly in groups, pointing at the information board and shrugging their shoulders.

'What's going on, Mum?' she said as her mother came back to her seat.

'They've cancelled our flight.'

Mixed emotions swam through Lorna's head. She had never wanted this holiday in the first place. Christmas was about carols and snow and the stocking at the end of the bed. She was embarrassed by her thoughts. Anyone would think she was six, like Emma, rather than sixteen but since Dad had moved out, and granny had moved in to help mum look after Emma, she had found herself clinging to her younger self: re-reading books she had read at primary school and sometimes reaching for her old bear at night.

'What are we going to do?'

'Wait. If the snow stops, there might be a flight in the morning. They are going to try and clear the runways.'

'But it's Christmas Eve. We can't stay here in the terminal on Christmas Eve!'

Marie brushed a strand of hair from Lorna's face and tried to pretend she hadn't seen her flinch. She just wished she could make her happy.

'We have no choice, Lorna. There's no traffic on the roads and the airport hotels will be full from the previous cancelled flights. We'll just have to make the best of it.'

'But what about Emma? What about her stocking?' Lorna waved frantically around her. 'Look at all these children. They can't spend Christmas Eve in an airport. They should be at home watching cartoons and singing awful Christmas songs and putting out sherry for Santa and...'

She stopped. Marie was looking at her, a strange expression on her face.

'Is that really what you think, Lorna? Is that what you would like yourself?'

Lorna gave a half-hearted shrug and then a nod. Marie thought how little she knew her daughter. 'I wish you'd told me. Look I promise we'll have a proper Christmas next year. The turkey, the carols, all the trimmings.'

Marie was aware of Jake moving back to his seat, a look of concern on his face. She bet he wished he'd never met her dysfunctional family.

Her phone beeped again.

'Is that Dad?'

Marie gave a pained look. 'Probably.'

'Couldn't you give him another chance, Mum?' she said. 'He's really sorry.'

Emma watched as a man with a neatly clipped white beard dressed in a navy blue uniform and matching cap strode over to two officials.

Before her mother could stop her, she had dropped her crayon and marched up to him, tugging at the gold braids on his sleeve.

'Emma…come back here!'

'Are you Santa?'

The man stared in surprise at the small girl. 'No. I'm Captain Davison.'

'Oh,' she said, disappointed. 'You looked like the Santa at the garden centre, except he was wearing a red coat and his beard was all big and fluffy. Do you fly the planes?'

'Yes, I do. Although, I won't be flying anywhere tonight. Why do you ask?'

Emma looked crestfallen. 'I was going to ask you to fly your plane and tell Santa where I am tonight.'

Marie rushed over, breathless and full of apologies, just as Emma held out a crumpled piece of paper. At the top, in thick pencil, she could just read the words: *from Emma at gatwic erport.* Underneath, the little girl had written her three Christmas wishes. As Marie led Emma back to her seat, she didn't notice Jake and Lorna stand up and make their way over to the group of officials.

Darkness had fallen. People lay where they could on benches or sat on the floor with their backs against their cabin bags. Outside the great windows, the snow fell softly to collect in drifts against the wheels of the planes.

'This is a passenger announcement. We have a very special visitor tonight. Would all parents with children please gather at the Christmas tree in the atrium.'

As Marie and her daughters reached the large fir at the bottom of the stairs, the overhead lights dimmed and hundreds of fairy lights twinkled from its dense green branches. Children clung to their parent's hands or ran around the red crepe-covered pot.

Marie was surprised to see Jake sitting with his guitar beneath the tree. Someone had rigged up a mike and amplifier. As he strummed his first chord, a hush fell on the crowd. His voice rang clear beneath the elevated ceiling of the terminal.

'Silent night…holy night.'

By his side, Lorna joined in. Marie touched her throat. When was the last time she had heard her shy daughter sing? One by one other voices joined in. Fathers and grandmothers and children. People brought together on this snowy Christmas Eve. The moment was magical.

Marie hesitated and then rummaged in her bag.

'What are you doing Mum?'

'I'm going to text Dad to wish him a happy Christmas and to invite him over for New Year.'

As the carol ended, a jingling of bells could be heard over the speakers and a large figure in red weaved his way through the crowd of children and their parents. 'Merry Christmas!' he boomed.

'So Santa got my Christmas wish list after all. He knew where I was – Captain Davison must have found him.'

Marie watched as Santa, with his neatly clipped beard and silver flight wings just visible beneath his red coat, handed out presents. She smiled at Emma and then glanced at Lorna.

'Yes,' She said. 'I think he must have.'

TOGETHER FOR CHRISTMAS

Julie put her hand over the mouthpiece of the phone.

'They want us to come over for Christmas.'

Kevin groaned but she made a shushing noise and turned her back to him. 'Yes, yes... of course we'd love to come. It's your turn after all.'

Ignoring the shaking of her husband's head, Julia paced the room, the phone wedged between her ear and her shoulder. 'No, of course there's not anything else we'd rather be doing, Christine. Christmas wouldn't be the same without you and Gary. After all it's what we've always done.'

She raised her eyebrows to her husband. 'Kevin? Yes of course he loves seeing you, too. Why wouldn't he?' She stifled a smile as Kevin held up his hand and started counting his fingers. He could obviously think of many reasons.

'We'll see you on the 25th then... as usual. No, I can't wait either. Look after yourself and give my love to Gary... Yes, I'll tell him.' She caught sight of her husband drawing a finger across his throat. 'Oh, and Kevin sends his love too.'

Placing the phone down on the receiver, Julie stood with her hands on her hips. 'I couldn't tell her.'

'Why ever not, Julie. It's easy enough. You just say, I'm sorry, Christine, but Kevin and I want to spend a quiet Christmas this year. Just the two of us.'

'But they've been our best friends for thirty years. We can't upset them.'

Her husband lowered his glasses onto the end of his nose and looked at her over the top of them. 'Just because we've spent every Christmas with them in the past, doesn't mean that we have to carry on doing it... especially now the children have all left home. It was different when we were younger and the children were little. It was fun then.'

'It's still fun.'

Kevin sniffed. 'If you call drinking a glass of sherry while Christine crucifies the turkey and Bing croons in the corner fun, then yes, it is.'

'I quite like sherry.'

'Well, I don't. It's bad enough having to bring a bottle as a present without having to drink it as well.'

Julie walked around behind Kevin and rested her chin on the top of his head. 'Oh, don't be like that. It's not so bad. Anyway it's nice not to have to do any cooking. Last year, when they came here, I spent the best part of a week planning the menu.'

'You didn't have to. It's only Christmas dinner after all. Meat and two veg at the end of the day.'

'Yes, I know that but it's what they expect — it's what I've always done. Christine's not much of a cook and it's nice for her to have something special.'

Kevin sighed. 'Well, I still wish you'd told her, Julie, while you had the chance.'

'It's not as easy as you think, you know.'

Julie knew that, whatever Kevin said, she'd done the right thing. Their friendship with Christine and Gary meant more to her than the prospect of a long read in bed Christmas morning, with a glass of bubbly, followed by a long walk over the downs with their Labrador, Trigger. No, they would have to spend their Christmas with their best friends as they always did.

'*I'll* do it.'

Julie stared at her husband. 'Do what?'

'I'll have a word with Gary. We men are better at this sort of thing, after all.'

She thought for a moment – maybe that wasn't such a bad idea. 'Well, alright then but be sensitive, Kevin. When were you thinking of talking to him?'

Her husband ran a hand through his hair then pushed himself out of his chair. 'No time like the present.'

Christine put down the phone. Gary stood in the doorway his eyebrows raised in a question.

'I couldn't do it.'

'No, I was listening.' He took off his glasses and wiped them on the hem of his T-shirt. 'What stopped you?'

She sunk into one of the armchairs by the fire. 'Our friendship, Gary. That's what stopped me.'

Her husband sat down opposite her and stroked his chin. 'But what about the talk we had last night? When we agree that this year we'd have Christmas abroad somewhere. Just the two of us.'

'I know what we agreed, but it's different when you have to actually say it.'

'You didn't start it very well by saying, *Are you still coming over to us for Christmas*? What did you expect her to say back?'

Christine sighed. 'I just wanted to check that was what they thought they were doing before I told her...'

'... that we don't want them to come,' Gary finished.

'It's not that – I love them both dearly. It's just that I think it would be nice to have a change.'

'It's not me you should be saying this to, is it?'

Christine threw a cushion at her husband. 'You're not helping. You should have heard her, Gary. She sounded so excited about it and I know how much they love coming here.'

'I just wish Kevin didn't always bring a bottle of sherry with him. I'd much rather drink beer.'

Christine stood up and stoked the fire. 'Well, that's obviously what he likes drinking at Christmas. Remember the year we went over to theirs and he had three different types.'

'Yes, and he insisted I try them all.' Gary made a face. 'I can still remember the taste.'

'It wouldn't be so bad if it wasn't my turn this year. Julie always makes such an effort and after the spread she put on last year, I feel we owe it to her to reciprocate.'

Gary looked horrified. 'You're not thinking of cooking those quails egg things like Julie did as a starter, are you?'

'Heaven forbid, no!' She leant forwards and lowered her voice. 'I really don't know why she does it. I'd rather just have melon. And why did she cook a goose? What's the matter with a plain old turkey?'

'I suppose she likes experimenting – after all it's what she does every other year... and you don't have to whisper, Chris. She can't hear you.'

'I know that... it's just that I hate saying these things. We sound so ungrateful... and disloyal.'

Christine reached over to the table next to her and picked up the silver-framed photograph that was standing there. It was of the four of them and had been taken on a shared holiday in Weymouth. They were all younger then and looked so carefree. Gary had more hair then as well.

Her eyes dropped to the holiday brochure on the coffee table. They'd thought about Tenerife or maybe Malta – somewhere warm and sunny. A Christmas to themselves... just for one year.

She put the photograph down and looked at Gary. 'There's nothing for it.'

'What do you mean?'

'You're going to have to do it, Gary.' She handed him her mobile. 'Arrange a drink with Kevin this evening and tell him.'

Gary took the phone from her. 'That's a good idea. The problem with you women is that you let sentiment get in your way.' He smiled to himself. 'Just think. A Christmas without sherry.'

But before he had a chance to punch in Kevin's number, the phone vibrated in his hand. His friend had got there first.

The doorbell rang somewhere deep inside the house as Julie and Kevin stood on the doorstep, stamping their feet to get some feeling back into them – it was a cold Christmas, colder than it had been in a long while.

As the door opened, Julie pasted a smile on her face and stepped forwards to hug her friend. 'Happy Christmas, Christine!'

Gary stood behind her and Kevin held out his hand to him. 'Great to see you, Mate.'

Julie watched him pump his friend's hand. Had she imagined it, or had the two of them exchanged a look?

'Glad you could come,' Gary said, his voice giving nothing away. 'Chris has been cooking the turkey since six, haven't you darling.'

'The turkey!' With a gasp, Christine dashed back into the house. 'I forgot to take it out.'

'I've brought these,' Julie said, as she and Kevin followed Gary into the house. 'Quails eggs. I know how much you both liked them last year and thought we could have them as a starter.'

Gary took them from her and lifted the lid of the Tupperware. 'Thanks. That's… um… great.'

'Oh, and *I've* something for you as well,' Kevin said, holding out the bottle he had in his hand.

She must have been imagining it, but Julie could have sworn her husband had just winked.

'Harvey's Bristol Cream,' he continued. 'Julie made me bring it but do you know what, Gary? I could really murder a beer if you have one.'

Gary took a bottle opener from the sideboard. He didn't seem at all bothered by the request. 'You bet. Won't be a minute.'

He left the room then came back in with the two beers and a bottle of Prosecco. Christine followed him in, her expression puzzled.

'I thought you ladies might like this for a change.'

'What a lovely idea.' Julie tried not to give her surprise away. This was definitely a break from routine. She took the glass that Gary held out to her. 'Thank you.'

She took a sip and when she raised her head, caught the nod Gary had just given her husband.

'I've just got to get something from the car, Julie,' Kevin said, putting down his glass.

'You have? What?'

'Oh, you'll see in a minute.'

Julie bent her head to Christina's. 'The two of them are acting very strangely.'

Christina looked over at her husband. 'I was just thinking the same thing,'

When Kevin returned, he had a bag in his hand. He reached inside and pulled out three presents wrapped in shiny blue paper. The smaller one he handed to Christina.

'Lovely ladies,' he said, with a smile. 'Forget the quail's eggs and the sherry, Kevin and I have some proper gifts... They're for all of us.'

'You have?' Julie stared at him in surprise. 'You never said.'

Kevin smiled. 'We don't have to tell you everything.'

Christine opened the present. It was flat and rectangular and when she took off the shiny paper, she saw it was an envelope. She opened it and a smile spread across her face. She showed Julie.

'It's a Christmas break for 2017 at that county house hotel we've been talking about for ages.'

Julie looked at Kevin. 'It's a wonderful present but you and Gary have never shown much interest in the place when we've talked about it.'

Kevin smiled. 'We might not show interest but that doesn't mean we don't take things in! It will give you both a break. We know it's hard work hosting Christmas.'

'There's a golf course and a spa,' Gary chipped in. 'And they even take dogs. Best thing is, though, we can spend time together but also have a bit of space to do things on our own as well.'

Julie put down her glass. She went over and kissed them both on the cheek. 'Thank you... both of you. It's a fabulous present. When did you concoct this idea?'

'It was when Gary and I went to the pub the evening Christina rang to discuss Christmas. See – we're not as useless as you think.'

'I never said you were.' She picked up one of the other presents. 'And what are these? These both look the same.'

'They are.' Kevin picked up the other and handed it to Christine. 'There's one for each family.'

Julie pulled off the paper and gasped. The book in her hands had *Christmas 1986-2016* in gold lettering on the front. She opened the cover and flipped through the pages. Inside, printed on shiny paper, was a photograph of every Christmas their two families had ever shared.

'Did you make this yourselves?'

'We used an online company,' Kevin said, looking pleased with himself. 'Gary scanned some of the old photos from the album and, for the newer ones, we just uploaded the pictures we'd saved on the computer. I took the laptop to the pub and we did it there so you wouldn't guess.'

Julie smiled to herself, remembering the shake of her husband's head when he'd come home from the pub that evening after meeting Gary. He'd gone to tell him that they wouldn't be spending Christmas with the two of them that year but hadn't been able to do it any more than she had.

She realised now it was because, in their hearts, neither of them had wanted to. What he and Gary had done, though, was much better.

'Well, I think its's fabulous.'

'And I do too,' Christina said.

The lights on the tree twinkled and Bing Crosby sang out from the speakers. The sherry stood unopened on the sideboard.

Julie lifted her glass and smiled at the others.

'To friendship,' she said.

'To friendship,' they all agreed.

ABOUT THE AUTHOR

Wendy Clarke lives in Sussex with her husband, cat and step-dog. She writes short fiction and articles for national magazines. You can find out more about Wendy on her blog:

http://wendyswritingnow.blogspot.co.uk

If you have enjoyed reading this collection of short stories, please consider leaving a review on Amazon.

Other books by Wendy Clarke that you may enjoy:

Room in Your Heart – A collection of romantic stories

She kept a special room in her heart. For a while, the door was locked and then, one day, she felt able to visit the room and realised that, instead of being a place to fear, it was full of happiness...

Room in Your Heart, is a collection of twelve romantic short stories of love and loss, previously published in The People's Friend Magazine. If you like stories with emotional depth and a satisfying ending then these stories will not fail to leave you unmoved.

The Last Rose – Stories of family and friendship

In his hand is the rose, as beautiful as I have ever seen – its creamy apricot petals curling inwards from his palm. He holds it out as one might a precious gift. 'The last rose is for you,' he says.

Printed in Great Britain
by Amazon

50483398R00095